ELEMENTAI

EARTH

ELEMENTAL FRACTIONS: EARTH
Cover artwork: 'Hands at the Cuevas de las Manos upon Río Pinturas, near the town of Perito Moreno in Santa Cruz Province, Argentina.' Original photograph taken by Mariano Cecowski. Public domain.

'The Watchers' © Maria Hummer
'Mother, Mother! The Dead are Coming After Me!' © Sasha Ravitch
'A Fox's Heart' © Wendy Ashley
'Blight of Spring' © Demian Lamont
'The Mountains like Waves' © Trish Marriott
'Tiny White Flowers' © Ivy Senna
'Legend' © Katarina Pejović
'Shadow on the Hill' © Liz Williams

All Rights Reserved Worldwide.

ISBN 978-1-915933-63-8

Except in the case of quotations embedded in critical articles or reviews, no part of this book may be reproduced or transmitted in any form or by any means, electronic or mechanical, including photocopying, recording, or by any information storage and retrieval system, without permission in writing from the publisher, unless that content is in the public domain.

A catalogue for this title is available from the British Library.

First published in 2024.
Asteria's Press
An imprint of Hadean Press Limited
59a Cavendish Street
Keighley, West Yorkshire
England

EARTH

Edited by
Erzebet Barthold & Lucy Greenwood

Contents

☙❧

Introduction *Lucy Greenwood*	vii
The Watchers *Maria Hummer*	1
Mother, Mother! The Dead are Coming After Me! *Sasha Ravitch*	9
A Fox's Heart *Wendy Ashley*	22
Blight of Spring *Demian Lamont*	32
The Mountains like Waves *Trish Marriott*	45
Tiny White Flowers *Ivy Senna*	58
Legend *Katarina Pejović*	67
Shadow on the Hill *Liz Williams*	84
About the Authors	94

Introduction

☙

There have been great societies that did not use the
wheel, but there have been no societies that did not
tell stories.
Ursula Le Guin

Imagine if we could take each element as a whole thought-form, and shine it through a prism, so that each of its qualities were separated into different components: fractions of a whole. The Magickal Women Conference has embarked upon creating a series of four anthologies connected to the elements of *Earth*, *Air*, *Fire*, and *Water*, in which each story is a fraction of one of these elements. This book you are holding in your hands is the first of these offerings; *Earth*.

Stories have been used as a tool to understand the world around us since time began, and are also an act of magic in themselves. The author creates worlds and universes, they distil the human experience and put down into words familiar feelings that we commonly share. Stories move the reader and invoke emotions and place a person in someone else's shoes. Fiction really is *magick*. For this collection, we have been blessed with submissions from authors from all over the world, in true Magickal Women Conference style, and we are very proud to showcase magickal thinking on an international scale. Our thanks go out to everyone who has submitted, contributed, and supported this project.

> I don't think there's really any difference between art –
> or writing, or music – and magic. And I particularly
> draw the link between magic and writing. I think that
> they are profoundly connected.
> *Alan Moore*

In this edition of *Elemental Fractions,* we have stories that explore the element of *Earth*. When compiling these stories, it was fascinating to see some overarching themes. There are sensory displays of earth throughout many of the stories, both nourishing and full of life, as well as those of ending, decay, and rebirth. There are boundaries that we make for ourselves or navigate from others, as well as an exploration of physical boundaries of the earth itself, from magical ridgeways of the English countryside to mysterious stone circles which help us explore our own place in time. There are absolute grounding emotions explored in this book, of loss and grief and love. Within these pages you will find science fiction, fantasy, magical realism and even some folk horror. It has been an absolute privilege to compile this anthology of diverse fiction, and I hope it will inspire and encourage more storytelling and magic, and perhaps even inspire you to have a go at weaving your own stories from the elements.

Lucy Greenwood

The Watchers

Maria Hummer

❦

Everyone in the village had a different name for them. My cousin called them the Archaeologists, due to the legend that they had once been men, researchers from another land, stricken to stone by local spirits before they could damage the land with their shovels, picks, and careless boots.

My mother called them the Guardians, because according to another legend they *were* local spirits, or perhaps had become so as part of their punishment. You could see them clearly from the window above our kitchen sink, and sometimes when my mother was washing up after dinner, I noticed her lips move soundlessly, her eyes glancing up the hill where the Guardians stood. If I ever did something to annoy her, like neglect to bring in the clothes from the line when there were dark clouds on the horizon, she would say, "Guardians give me patience," and turn her face plaintively in the direction of the stone circle.

My uncle Payton, her brother, simply called them the Lads; many an evening he spent sitting atop the one stone that had fallen on its side long ago in the time of cursed kings and questing knights, working his way through three bottles of golden ale, watching the sun go down over South Hinton.

I called them the Watchers, because from their position halfway up Grimble Hill they could see everything that went on in our village: from my mother at the kitchen sink, to the gossips standing in the open doorway of the church, to the weedy garden behind the Pheasant and Barrow, to the only bus stop within five miles, almost always sheltering old Mrs. Jenkins and her striped shopping bag on her way to or from visiting one of her many nieces. I liked thinking of these stone spirits as keeping a close eye on the petty disputes, triumphs, dangers, and domestic downfalls of the residents of South Hinton.

Naturally, the circle was a favourite play place for us children, and I became enamoured of these mysterious stones, even giving my heart to the shortest one when I was eight years old, taking him as my first husband with the other Watchers as witnesses to the solemn ceremony. I called him Henry and I knew, as only a child can know such a thing, that he loved me.

I knew this until the age of eleven when I foolishly shared the story with my friend Marvin, whom I'd come to trust almost as much as Henry. He broke my heart by saying with condescending authority, "You can't marry a *rock*," and I felt so ashamed that instantly all the magic was gone, all my beliefs, my faith in Henry. He became nothing more than the colourless, cold stone he was. Our marriage vows had been nothing but a silly little game, and so there would be no harm in letting Marvin put his sticky mouth on my neck while I leaned against the roughness of my never-was-husband. And that's exactly what happened.

*

Over the years, the Watchers eroded, were defiled and defaced, and eventually one of them even disappeared. It took a while for anyone to notice because, for some reason, most villagers had stopped visiting the stones, even my uncle Payton, who had taken to consuming his ale wherever he was most likely to provoke a blood-pounding argument (unfortunately for Mrs. Jenkins, this tended to mean the bus stop, and pesky questions about why she'd never had children).

The Watchers

I was probably the first to know the stone had disappeared, since even though I didn't visit them anymore I was still in the habit of gazing at them from the kitchen window. Everyone else simply scratched their heads and decided there must have always been four stones instead of five, but I knew better because the one that had vanished was Henry.

I had stopped going to the stone circle myself after that day with Marvin, and whenever my mother called upon them for patience, I would make fun of her for talking to rocks. At first, she defended herself, but over the years she grew quiet in the face of my bullying and eventually stopped mentioning them in my presence completely, opting instead for a perpetually wounded silence. I noted this as a triumph for my teenage self, and gloated that I had the power to make my own mother morose, this woman I had once believed more powerful and wise than anyone.

I didn't return to the stone circle until nearly ten years later, on the morning that I would be made Marvin's wife. Over the years, he had become something of the village favourite. There would be more than a few jealous tears shed at the sight of Marvin kissing me beneath my white veil, and the thought filled me with enough satisfaction (and, I thought, love) to accept his proposal. But I woke up on the morning of our wedding with a cold weight in my stomach like a stone, and I knew – like I had once known I had Henry's undying affection – that the feeling could only be resolved by visiting the Watchers.

I proceeded up the hill, impulsively, in my bare feet, which I soon regretted because the field around the Watchers was liberally decorated with excrement, mostly from sheep but also dogs and foxes, many of these deposits still alarmingly fresh, or perhaps just appearing so after a long night soaking in countryside dew. I managed to avoid stepping in anything loathsome, but it meant that my progress up the hill was meandering and slow – much like my own life, I bitterly thought.

I made it to the circle and sat upon the horizontal stone where uncle Payton had used to drink with the Lads. I pulled my bare feet onto its cold surface and held my knees close, gazing down at the sleepy insufferable village I'd only left in my life once, just once, for a duck egg festival somewhere on the coast.

I could see the village church from my vantage point among the rocks; someone was arranging baskets of white tulips on either side of the church door. My wedding dress was freshly pressed and waiting for me in my mother's sewing room. Marvin wouldn't be awake yet; he was sleeping off a riotous evening with friends in the Pheasant and Barrow.

I hadn't any notion of what I might do in the stone circle besides cry, but the shit-dodging journey uphill had transformed all trace particles of melancholy into annoyance. I tried to recover the sadness that had driven me up there, and couldn't find it anymore. It was gone.

I sighed and leaned back on the rock with my palms flat behind me. I tilted my chin up until I couldn't see the village anymore, yet there it was swimming perpetually in my mind, along with the faces of every person I had ever known. There was my father, growing ever more discouraged at the daily crossword puzzle until finally he'd snap at something unrelated I had done. And there was my mother, sitting at the dinner table in her newfound coldness, tightening her mouth at my restless hands and my conversational interruptions. Then there was Marvin, entering our home or the church or the Pheasant and Barrow to cracking smiles and pats on the back. He made my parents grin in a way I no longer could, and they approved of his rigid posture and his well-meaning jibes at my various unforgiveable flaws: I was too daydreamy, too impulsive and careless and naïve, and he was going to see to it that I lived a good life because heaven knows I could barely handle tying one shoe without forgetting to tie the other. He loved me for my hopelessness, which I thought meant he loved *me*, but I was starting to see that what he really loved was his own pragmatism and how it shone out in contrast to my inconsistencies. Perhaps he was marrying me in order to feel indispensable. Perhaps what he really loved was his own usefulness.

An idea was emerging in my being, some truth that felt almost like it was emanating into my hands and my heart from the stone I was sitting on. I began to see that everyone felt so warmly toward Marvin because you always knew who you were with Marvin, or at least who you were supposed to be, because he would tell you. This is what happened every time he refused to put sugar in my tea, or laughed when I told him a dream I'd had, or indeed when he kissed me on that fateful day in front of my once-beloved Henry.

I watched a magpie fly overhead, looking as frustrated as I felt. I wondered what had rustled it, grumbling, from its nest. Its wing feathers looked like fingers to me, and I wondered what it must feel like to hold such freedom literally in the palm of your hand. My own fingers began to itch at the thought of having feathers, and when I brought my hand in front of my face to scratch it, lowering my gaze from the sky, there was a man I'd never seen before standing in front of me.

"Hello," he said in a pleasantly scratchy voice. His clothes were brown and plain, but clean, and his dark hair fell in curls down to his chin. He was either oblivious to the fright he had given me, or was choosing to pretend it hadn't happened. Either way, I was grateful that he wasn't grinning and poking my sides like Marvin might have done, crowing with pleasure, "Did I frighten you?"

"Nice day," said the stranger, "but windy. Can't light a cigarette in this field so I thought I'd try behind one of these rocks. You don't mind, do you?"

"No, of course not," I said. I found it funny but also strangely touching that my opinion of whether he should smoke in the stone circle actually counted for something. It wasn't my field; it wasn't anybody's, really, except for the moaning sheep and the magpies and the Watchers themselves.

He fished a cigarette out of his pocket and lit it in the shade of the tallest stone, then he went to stand and smoke in the empty space where Henry had used to be.

In fact, his height was very close to what I remembered Henry's being. If I stood nose to nose with him, and threaded my arms beneath his…

"Remind you of someone?" he asked. There was a trace of a smile in his lips, but not a mocking one, more like he was genuinely flattered by the idea that I might find him familiar.

"Sorry," I said. "Perhaps you do. But I've never seen you before, have I?"

"It's not my first time passing through South Hinton," he said, "though it has been a fair few years. You would have been a mere young lass, by the look of it."

"And you?" I asked, for he didn't look much older than I was, perhaps twenty-three.

"I'm older than I seem."

"How old?"

But he didn't answer. He just smoked in silence, gazing downhill.

Suddenly conscious that I was wearing only my nightdress and an old cardigan of my father's for warmth, I gathered the fabric around my knees. Marvin would be waking soon. My father would be out checking the strawberries. Even old Father

Lloyd might be pacing the churchyard, practicing his sermon, and what would any of them think if they saw me with a strange man in the stone circle on my wedding day, barely half-dressed?

"There seems to be a to-do going on down the church," said the man. "Someone you know getting married?"

"Yes," I said, but would admit nothing further than that.

"Weddings always make me nostalgic," he said. "I was betrothed myself, once. Why, we were as good as married. But one day, she just seemed to forget all about me, like none of it had ever happened. I was so ashamed, I left town, and I've been wandering ever since."

He laughed lightly, chiding himself, in the silence that followed. "Forgive me. I talk too much. Starved for conversation, I suppose. I'll be quiet now."

He smoked while I sat there, heart pounding. Surely it was a coincidence, everything he said, his height, the way he stood in Henry's old place like it was the most natural thing in the world.

"What's your name?" I asked. He looked at me curiously, and I added, "In case I should run into someone who knows you."

"It's Clive. Yours?"

"Loretta."

"Loretta," he repeated, almost with a sigh. "It's strange. I feel like I knew that. The instant you said Loretta... I knew it was right."

We were silent again. The stone I sat on was becoming quite painful beneath me, and I knew I would have to move soon. But I didn't move. I stayed very still, thinking about what Clive had said, thinking about that knowing. How all creatures knew when it was time to stand, time to sit, time to fly. How did we know such things? And how could it be possible to ignore them, as I seemed to have been doing for a very long time?

Clive stubbed out his cigarette and was left with nothing to do with his hands. He looked around, as if searching for something else he could grasp, like a stick, a soft arm, a thread of meaning. He settled for cracking his knuckles, one after the other.

"Mind if I sit with you?" he asked.

"I'll be going in a moment."

"That's alright. Then we'll have a moment."

He settled down beside me and I shivered, though the sun was now showering profusely down upon us, like grains of rice would be showered on me not two hours from now. His hand landed on the rock next to mine, and slowly shifted and spread until his warm, dry palm covered all of my fingers. My whole body thrummed, like the triumphal reverberations in a church for the split second after an organ has stopped sounding.

"I'm the one getting married," I confessed.

He nodded. He did not move his hand. We sat there with the wind and the sun between us, the silence broken only by the dissatisfied call of a magpie. I wanted it to shut up and fly away but it stayed there, calling, calling, trying desperately to make itself heard.

Mother, Mother! The Dead are Coming After Me!

Sasha Ravitch

☙

Ad regem Eumenidium et reginam eius: Gwynn ap Nudd qui es ultra in silvis pro amore concubine tue permitte nos venire domum

To the King of the Spirits and his queen: Gwyn ap Nudd, you who are yonder in the forest, for the love of your mate, permit me to enter your dwelling.
14th Century Latin Manuscript

Night comes in black as the spaces between your teeth and dripping its hot pitch across the earth; it slouches slowly, tar-pit dragging long and hard and thick as butter churned one too many times. She went to bed nervous, knowing what tonight was, just as she had gone to bed nervous knowing what this night was her entire life. She was raised on the tales, suckled at the teat of hearth-side storytelling, eyes wide like bloated moons twisted up ever higher into the mouth of the sky as visions both grotesque and awe-ful were conjured fire-side. Grandparents whispering what their grandparents had told them, her older cousins grabbing her wrist when she got too close to the window.

She remembered how the air *tasted* on those nights: cold as sky-iron having fallen into a holy well, and saturated with choking, thick black smoke which spun up like charcoal snow flurries from the pounding of invisible hooves. She remembered how the air *felt* on those nights: like it might cleave itself into so many aerial slits around her and suck her into the distended belly of forever. These memories of the *nights before,* so many star spackled canopies of antecedent years, played across the velvet curtain of her closed eyes as she fell asleep. She could hear, through her closed window, a woman in the neighborhood whimpering out in terror. The nearby woman's grief-stricken echo spilled her secret to the whole neighborhood: she had heard the howls of *His* hounds, and her family would tend to her limp body in the morning.

Quite suddenly, she was *aware*. It is a strange thing, too, to be so aware of dying. Not in the abstract, philosophical sense – no pipe-smoking armchair pulpitizing. Nor was this some morbid poet's musing, something as rapturous and delusional as light reflecting off the surface of still water. No, this was a practical and immersive presence in the process of putrification. She simply knew she was dead, that she was in *this state of death*, that she was dead as a *verb* and not *just a noun*, as she had formerly only been acquainted. She was struck, in fact, by the lack of grandeur and mystery it presented in its profound stillness, gone were the anxieties of mortality and the fallible, clinging desire to life. She did not find herself wracked with anxiety, with panic, with remorse. There were no regrets that obscured her vision like a sudden snow flurry. Perhaps there were no emotions at all; yes, she felt no feelings, no internal sensorium in response to this condition. But perhaps that would pass, that the ambient malaise and casualness would soon be replaced by some virulent and protesting frenzy. After all, she had only *just* become aware of her deadness.

As her mind became familiarized with the precept of her morbidity, she was struck by the relative surprise of her consciousness. Well, conditional consciousness. She strained to recall her final moments pre-death, and yet she could not conjure to mind anything remotely salient. There were some phantom clues, a bread-crumb trail of voices calling out her name – not to catch her attention, no, and not with the acute urgency of preventative calling. No, this was…a distant, mournful hymnal, this was the aching, preternaturally grief-shaped midnight call of the loon on the lake. This was – *a search party*. A few fragmented scenes played out across the dappled veil of darkness: feeling the rough, cracked bark of an ancient oak, how it chafed against the softness of the pads of her fingers; a scent of peat-smoke, of some fire which smoldered in the felled leaves and the rotting logs. There was the sensation of being sucked into, pulled under, surrounded by a harsh descending wind; the dissonant choral melody of hounds growling, barking, howling in fury and awe alike. Yes, *and of course*, the darkness – she remembered the darkness of this, a darkness not at all unlike the one she now found herself within. A familiar but different thing; shades of anhedonic vantablack, incapacitated by the shrillness of crises.

Her heart hitched slightly at the recollection of these memories, piecemeal as they may have been; she recognized, now, on some fundamental and pre-conscious level, that she may not have just simply fallen asleep at a ripe old age and drifted off to whatever was beyond, whatever was *out there*. Had she been lost? Had she been taken? *Why had her heart hitched if she was dead?* For the first time since she had regained consciousness, an emotion – and awfully embodied thing, a thing which crept up from her guts, slowly stirring, and ricocheting out in waves of tingles to her fingertips, to the crown of her head – emerged inside her head. *Panic*, she thought, recognizing the sort of roiling dizziness and peripheral nausea, and the revivifying shock to the system of adrenaline flooding back into her presumably immobilized form. *How have I died? Where did I die?* Had she wandered off, or had she been taken? She squirmed as the question slinked up her spinal cord to wrap neatly 'round her neck – the constant reminder of the noose of awareness.

And then she realized that she had squirmed, she had *moved!* As if in some countering response, she froze once more: *do the dead move?* She felt relatively sure that in absolutely none of the literature, none of the scientific studies, none of the basic biology classes she had taken or any of the baroque and gothic horror she had allowed herself to read, had a dead person suddenly being able to move their body *ever* been a good thing. A gentle internal scream wafted around the closed cave of her mouth. Instinctually, and with absolutely no coherent or rational thought, she began to flail – expecting to be met with the sateen walls of a coffin, or perhaps the moist, fecund mold of soil. But the sensation she encountered was entirely different: a viscous, smooth, sopping wetness and sort of rough bed of flesh. She could feel the slickness, the gentle rancor of a still, damp riverbed beneath her body, coating her back and legs in its gentle stickiness. She flung her arms out desperately, to feel out her surroundings, trying to suss out the location of her new carceral void. Smooth, polished prison-bars that tapered off to devastating points, leviathan-like lances which could rend stone and till a forest floor. She cautiously, ever-so slowly, slipped forward and allowed her toes to reach out and – *fangs!* She recoiled. She had found herself buried inside a mouth: the mouth of, what appeared to be, a giant serpent.

She screamed and it felt as if the world broke around her, the echo of her duress bouncing off the wet-ribbed tunnel of this beast's mouth, stirring it from whatever dormant rest it had fallen into since inviting her into its gullet. She dragged herself forward, clinging to the fringes of a split tongue like frayed rope, grabbing onto gigantic needle-teeth, thrusting herself through the sour emulsive territory of the mouth until she reached those fangs once more. Desperately, eagerly, with perhaps more courage than she had known in her life, she wailed and wailed and attempted to pry open the grotesque ophidian birdcage which barricaded her escape. And then she felt it – *felt* the *sound*, a slow curdling rumble from deep, deep down and very, very far, rising like a roll of thunder from the distant belly of the beast that she had found herself buried in, rolling toward her and raising from faraway murmur to a deafening explosion. As the wave of the roar crashed upon the shore of her body, she was slammed against the teeth – and then, quite suddenly and all at once, there was an onslaught of movement. She felt herself falling sideways as the serpent unclenched its jaw to allow the sound of its displeasure to escape and was met with a sensation of flesh being seared – of being flayed open. Fangs punctured her abdomen, penetrating the soft mass of her belly, plunging deep into the fluttering chaos of her viscera. One fang, in particular, dragged across her abdomen, creating a leyline of bloodied, gnarled mess. There was a sudden squishing, slopping, tugging sensation – and she realized her insides were falling outside of herself; her organs were bulging out of the new mouth torn into her belly, like a tongue dragging between its lips. At last the teeth seemed to disengage from her desecrated flesh, giving way to a new wave of darkness. She braced herself for some inevitable fall into a strange vacuum-void.

Instead, however, she was swiftly buried beneath a gritty, moist womb of soil. The loamy earth held fast around her, quickly filling in the errant crevices of her body, and seeming to suck the remaining oxygen out of her lungs. An undulating cascade of vibrations informed her the serpent, this giant subterranean wyrm, was slowly slithering below ground, away from her, perhaps in some tunnel it had already burrowed, while she remained within the bed of mulch from the capsized enclave. She opened her eyes, feeling her lashes struggle against the dirt, unfurling as a hand unclenching after having held a fist for far too long. In the darkness of her surroundings, half-asphyxiated as she was, she felt as if she were gazing at the sky of stars. *Am I dying again?* She had already died once, hadn't she? And yet now she found her body flex and writhe in aspiration of air, each attempt at breath met by a sporadic spasm, an unseemly tremor, the feeling of being swallowed by a new mouth: that of the earth. Her toe twitched, catching on the tendrilous fingers of some tree's roots. The darkness gave way to another darkness, and her eyes once more closed.

Consciousness, again. Squirming slightly at the crushing pressure seeming to envelop her from all sides, she resigned herself to attempting escape. Heaving and thrusting, her exhausted muscles resisting the crushing temptation to surrender, she managed to force both arms above her head and loosen some of the more compact soil around her. In the spaces her movements made, dirt shook free like small dustings of snow, and she felt an earth worm – desperate to get away from her – wriggle against the taut skin of her grasping hands. Clawful of dirt by clawful of dirt, with painful thrust and churn of the hips and taut leveraging of the legs, she ascended to the surface. She felt where the gloaming surface level silt became aerated, pock-marked with the roots of whatever life had survived the winter frost and formed a cold crust which she had to pound apart with her knuckles. But it worked, and oxygen pooled in fast and sweet to sting her lungs as they expanded.

She twisted her head to the side, and peering through the perforated veil of earth, she swore she saw something glittering below ground – a heaving glass structure, something with the

Mother, Mother! The Dead are Coming After Me!

luminous interiority of stars wrought into royal architecture. Before she could endeavor to squint and refine her vision, pain cracked through her body as a whip would, and she felt her shoulder dislodge from its very same socket. Some alien hand, strange as it was strong and cold as corpse-breath, had latched itself around her wrist and was heaving her out of the earth with an unrelenting vice-grip. Her body broke free, birthed from the winter-fetid womb of frozen decay, and was flung into the air. She seized, suspended in the night, time caught in amber, and gravity eliminated. And then she fell, hard, body wrapping around the flexed haunches of a large, galloping black horse. As she began to slip, naturally bucked off by the feral gallop of the creature, she was caught by that same dislocated arm and pinned down by a leather strap around her mutilated torso, which continued oozing a viscous sludge of blood and dirt and bile with the momentum of the stampede.

On and on they seemed to ride, through the sky, through the forest saturated with frigid, boney trees and snaggle-toothed shrubs whose vines and brambles tore at her skin and ripped tangles of her hair from her scalp. On and on they seemed to ride, through dead leaves and across rivers of blood, atop rain clouds and down lightning bolts, a swarming mass of ululating figures in their fractious tribes, with billowing black cloaks and faces masked in nebulous shadow, their declarative cries piercing the night as their elf-shot struck all those unwitting passersby. On and on they seemed to ride, the white hounds with their red ears and eyes howling relentlessly into the invisible horizon. On and on they seemed to ride, slowly amassing new souls, both living and freshly dead, growing ever more into a flooding mass of convulsing bodies, a discordant symphony of moans and growls, or pleading prayers, of bleating cries, of hands grabbing desperately for disparate branches that they might hang on tightly enough to be sucked out of the avalanching throng. And still, the thick smell of peat-smoke and blood baiting the wind and perfuming it with an acrid stench. And still, they rode, on and on, for miles and years.

The trooping swarm came to an abrupt stop, nearly colliding into themselves within a large starry alcove in the middle of an unfamiliar woods. She succeeded in stretching her neck just far enough to the left to bear witness to a leviathan of an Oak Tree: as old and alive as anything, with its serrated bark teeth grinning at her, and the ossified tentacles of its branches reaching out with an unkind glee. She shuddered, the phantom gleam of otherworldly armor from such peculiar knights glinting in her periphery. What a queer glow seemed to illuminate this sordid party of night-creatures; as if the ghost-lights fluttered in a petulant obeisance like lanterns to those who commanded the frightful horde. She attempted to lay limply on the back of the steed, recalling instructions around playing dead as a protective defense against predators. But she knew the torrential racing of her heart and the sharp choking breaths of air she kept dragging deeper into her unraveling spool of a body betrayed her.

An unidentifiable number of hands configured around her abdomen, heaving her from the horse's haunches and half-dragging, half-carrying her to the base of the Oak. The chitinous clatter of otherworldly armor felt mellifluous, violent in the otherwise abominable silence of the night, and she held her breath as she was released, collapsing onto the forest floor and banging her knees against gangly roots. She huddled in on herself, trying to push body organs back into the bruised carapace of her torso, and feebly holding the dislocated arm which dangled like a fishing line from her shoulder. What was the point? She found herself wondering. *I'm not leaving this place, anyway.*

It was then that He descended from horseback – the echo of

his boots landing upon the earth quieting all the errant entities whispering amongst themselves. He was at once formidably giant, and yet lithe and delicate – a figure fashioned from as much solid black marble as he had been woven from silk. She presumed he was a He, but it was all together impossible to distinguish features from where she was, for he was cloaked in a shadow of endless black light, or, perhaps, an anti-light, through which a swirling cavalcade of miniature spectral orbs danced endlessly across his visage like stars floating upwards into an overturned cauldron. As he slowly approached her, his form distorted further into an elongated mass of fibrous obsidian, crowned by the many-spoked tridents of giant antlers. The crowning brambles of his antlers were threaded with a series of vermillion pulsating, winding threads that held a litany of tiny red stars suspended through them. Her eyes widened in an involuntary awe at the grotesque beauty of this Dark Rider, of his soot-skin and his black clothes, of his blistering red eyes and the vague impression of crooked lips, of the starry-crown of blooded night which adorned his preternaturally still head.

He paused in front of her, looming with an equivalent intimidation as the Oak to her back. With a silent motion, he signaled to a series of spirits within his retinue, who immediately began to shuffle toward her. He stepped away, and she reflexively attempted to scuttle away from the figures moving toward her. She was too weak, though, and her body too feeble, and they had soon set themselves upon her, dragging her upside down up the tree just enough for her respective legs to be tied to opposing branches, and knotted with a thick green cord which kept her hanging, suspended, in some inverse crucifixion. Staccato whimpers erupted from her ripped lips, but no mind was paid by the attendant Beings, who secured her and began to depart. There she hung, what blood remained rushing to the gently swinging pendulum of her head, limp arms dragging on the ground beneath her, the pounding pain obscuring her vision as now, more figures approached.

The acute sting of fresh lacerations rang out through her flesh as countless tiny black blades plunged in the churning slop of her abdomen. Small, quick hands seemed to reach around her insides, rooting around like truffle pigs, and seamlessly ripping, tearing, shredding, pulling, knotting, twisting, and rearranging the entire internal world of her viscera. It no longer hurt – not in a way that she may have been able to compare to any other pain she had experienced previously, at least – if it hurt, it was in such a distinctively unusual way that the curiosity at its peculiarity overwhelmed the body's response to potential discomfort. The sounds were what stood out: the suckling, the squelching, the suction-slapping pops, the puckering and sliding, the bursting of blood-bubbles, the popping of cartilage, the crackling of gristle. She observed as if under some depersonalizing anesthesia, having left her body just enough to witness the swift fists buried deep in the terra of her guts. Every so often, some peculiar organ would come toppling out of the open wounds and fall to the rotting mulch below, only to be lifted up and re-inserted into the gaping mouth of her midriff.

There was one last, heaving tug – and out popped a round, reddish gray mass of tissue from somewhere above the ophidian garland of her intestines. She watched as one of the creatures – his gnarled, twisted face obscured by a thick hood from his cape, made a sort of chittering noise of satisfaction. That sticky, ruddied organ was slipped into a cloth sack made of green wool, and the goblin scampered off to hand the bag to the giant Dark Man with his horns-of-hart and his ivory-hounds. He affixed the bag to his horse, and then approached her once more. This time, he came closer still, and she could feel the radiant heat of his body singe her lashes. Then he was reaching, ripping her from the tree, and holding her up to him by her neck. A bullroar built up from his belly and broke the dam of his lips, a ferocious and harrowing howl that morphed into a laugh of unprecedented, cunning glee. The bellowing, pounding sound of his laughter shot through her body and ricocheted off of her teeth, off of the skeletal remains of her figure, into the empty spaces of her redesigned body. And with the hand *not* holding her up by her neck, he plucked one of the red stars from the mantle of his antlered crown, and ruthlessly shoved his star-clutching fist into her guts, placing this new pulsar in the same space where the former organ had been removed.

She felt a blinding shock of electrical heat cauterize her guts from the inside out and send her body into convulsive shivers of ecstasy, and then she was being pushed against the trunk of the Oak tree. The tree split open and swallowed her into a chute in the base of its trunk, shooting her through the myriad tunnels from whence she had attempted to escape the subterranean serpent, earlier. Faster and faster, past the glass castle, until she spotted the protruding fangs of an open mouth with a forked tongue grinning at her.

When she awoke, the cold face of the Sun was glowering a warmth-less light upon her spent and splayed body. Her eyes struggled to open, but eventually she was able to distinguish her surroundings as a nearby field adjacent to her house. She weakly clutched at her belly, expecting to feel a motley bouquet of flesh and guts, but was roused to greater wakefulness by shock: she felt no open wounds, no slithering rivulets of blood. With an aching thrust, she pulled herself up, and examined herself: she remained in the same night dress she had fallen asleep in the previous evening, seemingly unchanged except for several stains from the dirt and grass she must have fallen asleep upon. All that appeared out of the ordinary could have been easily explained away by the consequences of some unusual episode of sleepwalking, or an aberrant reaction to a very visceral nightmare. Feeling slightly disoriented, and all the more embarrassed, she made her way back home with the dawn light, hoping to sneak into the bath prior to any of her family awakening.

When she arrived at the family home, she paused. The window to her bedroom was open, and she knew she had locked it before slumber – as was always the tradition on nights as renowned as the previous one had been. Shaking her head, she proceeded forward. She entered through the unlocked back door of the home, and staggered to the washroom, where she began to prepare a bath. Disrobing, she began to enter the steaming tub before something caught her attention in her periphery – her reflection in the washroom mirror. Slowly, heart hitched in her throat like a fish caught on a hook, she turned, to witness her naked reflection.

And that was when she saw it: the red tails of comet-like streaks across the torso of her body, evidence of the blades that had entered and the fangs which had pierced. The wounds did not look fresh, they did not feel raw, there was no trace of blood or the stinging chafe of scabs, only these striking scarlet streaks across the moonlight of her body. And there, right where the organ had been stolen, right where the star had replaced it, a strange red burn that reminded her so much of a beauty mark. Shaking, she reached for the same shoulder blade her arm had been dislocated from and felt the distinct searing pain of bruises and stretched tendons. *It was real*, she uttered in disbelief. She tenderly allowed herself to descend into the tub of hot water. She leaned back, and closed her eyes, only to be immediately swallowed by a vision of His face: that dark, grinning face, with those antlers so massive they scraped the stars from the sky and tangled them up in their velvet, the feeling of his fists clenched around her flesh, and one thought soldered into the lining of her skull: *You shall know me as your Master, and we will ride again at dark.*

A Fox's Heart

Wendy Ashley

ॐ

It doesn't look as I'd expected. It's a small, desiccated thing, barely the size of a plum. More like a prune, and hardly that.

I thought at least she would have cared for it better. But there had been no silk wrapping or velvet cushion, just a nest of brittle, yellowing newspaper, dark brown stains obscuring much of the newsprint. And she'd chosen a Huntley and Palmer's biscuit tin to hide it in, so what should I have expected? My sentimental heart was running away with me again. She'd always warned me about that.

Assorted Creams, Superior Reading Biscuits. I'd struggled to open the tin. Traces of soil clinging to it still. The lid was dented, the yellow roses printed there, scratched and faded and speckled with rust. Years spent in the back of the shed, beneath cans of dried-up old paint and empty flowerpots, as if it was worth no more than a spanner or a jar of screws. Something to be forgotten, not worth remembering.

I don't know how she could have thought that. Perhaps it was easier that way.

*

I first saw the fox under Nan's plum tree in her garden. I loved that garden as a child, with its apple trees, roses and snapdragons, the laurel full of sparrows, and the path by the washing line where I bounced my tennis ball. But I hated the plum tree. It was where the wasps were.

You wouldn't have known, not at first. You had to get close to hear their buzzing, but by then it would be too late.

Nan found me there once, frozen beneath the tree with a windfall still held in my hand. Five or six wasps buzzed persistently about me, daring me to move as I held myself rigid, tears sliding down my cheeks, breath gasping, knowing I couldn't hold out much longer. I was going to have to run. I was going to have to scream and run and wave my arms, and the wasps would get angry and chase and sting me.

"Drop the plum, dear," she'd said, walking calmly to my side, not flinching as the wasps began circling her too. "Come on now, let's get some squash, eh?"

Putting a soft, warm arm around my shoulders, she guided me steadily and determinedly back to the house. She flipped the tea-towel in her hand at the wasps as they began to follow, and they went away.

The fox had been as fearless of the wasps as my Nan. It appeared one bright afternoon, nosing in the long grass beneath the plum tree, munching on fallen fruit. I'd watched amazed from where I sat near the rose bed, hidden, I thought, by the shadows. I loved the brightness of its fur and the way the sun gleamed off it like fire. Its right ear was a little ragged and missing a tip and I winced when I saw the wasps closing in around its head. But it just shook itself and carried on foraging.

When finally, it did lift its head, it looked straight to where I was, as if it had known I was there all that time. Its amber eyes were clear and sharp and not a bit afraid. It stared at me for a second or two, then casually turned and moved towards where the garden fence disappeared behind the old shed. Slipping between the two it vanished out to the streets beyond.

When I told my mother about it, she'd just grimaced. "Oh God, nasty creature. You stay away from it Grace. You hear me?"

But I saw my Nan's face and the gleam in her eyes. It struck me as a kind of excited sadness. "Don't fuss so, Laura," she said. "He's alright."

*

When we hide things, do we really understand who we're hiding them from and why? Are we protecting ourselves or others? And if we forget what was hidden, what then? How do we find it again?

The change came slowly at first and it had been easy to miss. It is not a forgetting so much as a losing. Except she hadn't understood what she was losing, just that something was terribly wrong, and no one was to know. Especially me.

She was strong, stubborn, and determined. She looked after herself, cooked all her own meals, dug in the garden and chopped wood for her fire. She climbed ladders and rewired plugs, baked cakes for the church fête, and checked in on ninety-three-year-old Mrs Lewis at the end of her road who couldn't get out so much anymore. And when I visited, she took care of me too. So even though I noticed it starting I didn't want to believe it. The limp that came and went in her left leg, the blankness that flickered occasionally in her grey eyes when I asked her a question, the stumble over a word or the wrong name given to an item. All were shaken off as nothing, or a bit of silliness. She was a magician in her misdirection, and I let her do it.

It was when she called me by my mother's name, then cried at her error, that I really began to accept that something bad was coming.

*

A Fox's Heart

The fox is in the garden.

I know it's still there. I can see the orange blur of its presence distorted through the wobbly glass of the bathroom window. I know where it is, I know what it's doing, and it worries me, leaves me uncertain.

I think Nan knows it's there as well. She moans softly as I wash her back and I can't tell if she's frightened or confused. Perhaps it's neither. Perhaps what I take as a moan of distress is nothing more than a sigh, an acknowledgement that she's alive and tired and wishes that this would all be over soon. Which is sadder – fear of life, or boredom of it?

The knobs of her spine protrude almost like teeth through the paper-thin tissue of her skin. I skim the flannel down again, rinsing the soap away and whisper condolences to her shivering head. The grey hair is so thin now I can see the pink of her scalp and the shape of her skull. I don't know when she became so old.

"Ok Nan?" I say, wiping her face. "Feel better now?"

A foolish thing to ask, but she doesn't seem to hear me. Her thoughts are elsewhere, if anywhere at all. Perhaps she's thinking about the fox, its sharp snout pushing at the earth where she'd been digging earlier, her fingernails clawing at the dank earth beneath the plum tree.

She'd been kneeling there, in the rain, head bowed, shoulders shaking as she scrabbled in the wet earth with her bare hands. No coat, feet bare, just her favourite flannelette nightie to protect her and it was now soddened, moulded around her diminished form.

I'd run across the lawn cursing myself for not having come sooner, and cursing Mrs Hurd her neighbour for letting this happen, while knowing there was no blame to be attached. Just my terrible error, for thinking that Nan would be fine and not accepting the truth. This was not one of life's hiccups, this was it. Nan was old, struggling and never going to be herself again.

"Nan? Nan! What are you doing?"

Her shoulders were shockingly cold. It was like touching bone, as if the rain had washed all her flesh away.

"Nan?"

I tightened my grip on her shoulders, feeling the grind and effort of their movement, but still she kept on digging, scrabbling at the mud, earth black beneath her nails. Horrified I saw there were deep scratches across the back of her hands. Thin pink rivulets ran from them and dripped from her fingers, mixing with the mud in the hole.

"Nanna, come on. Stop it now. Stop. Please!" I tried grabbing at her hands, but she screamed and slapped me away.

"No, Laura! Leave me!"

"It's Grace, Nanna. Not her. It's me, her daughter. Gracie."

"Get off me!"

"Gracie, Nan. Remember? You know I was coming. I always come. It's our Saturday. Stop now, come on. Every Saturday, for our weekend. It's our weekend Nanna."

She hesitated. "Grace?" One mud caked finger tentatively touched my nose as recognition flickered in her pale eyes. Then, with a sob, she turned back to the earth and the task she'd set herself.

"No, Nan. Stop!"

"I can't find it Gracie. I can't find it. I have to give it back. I promised."

"Find what? There's nothing there. Stop Nan, please. Stop!"

I grabbed at her hands again and fought to hold them still. She gave a small cry then finally gave in, her body sagging back into my embrace as her strength sapped away.

"I didn't mean to forget, darling."

"It's ok."

"But it hurt so much."

I didn't know what to say. I could only kiss her cold, wet hair, and hold her close.

"Everything is going to be fine, Nan," I lied, and hooking my hands under her armpits, I heaved us both out of the mud.

"It hurt so much, I tore it out," she said. "But he brought it back to me. How could I lose it again? You understand?"

I guided her arms through the sleeves of a fresh, dry nightie and gently tugged the warm material over her swaying body. She seemed so empty and frail. I wanted to tell her no, I didn't understand. How could I when this seemed to have happened so quickly? I was going to have to call a doctor. She would hate me for it.

"I loved him. I owe him, Gracie."

I sat her on the edge of her bed then eased her legs under the covers. Anger flared within me. She didn't owe him anything.

"He left you, Nan. It wasn't your fault."

She shook her head, pushing back as I tried to lay her down.

"No. I left him. Don't you see. We knew we couldn't, but … I left him."

"Grandad left you. Remember? He buggered off and left you with no money and a two-year-old daughter to bring up by yourself. God's sake! You don't owe him anything!"

I catch myself and stop struggling with her. I can feel the tears starting and I don't want to cry in front of her. It will only distress her more. Why does it matter anyway? I should just let her believe what she says. Come tomorrow we'll probably have to start this all over again.

But to my surprise, she begins to laugh. A big sound that should no longer fit in the brittle cage of her chest. In that moment she sounds like herself again.

"No! Not him, you silly girl. Not that stupid man."

But then her tears come, and it is all I can do not to join her.

"Stupid," she sobs. "Stupid, stupid, stupid."

*

Grief is a very personal thing. There is no fixed path to follow, no guide to find your way through it. All any of us can be sure of is there will be pain.

She kept a faded photo of her parents in a silver frame on her bedside table. The smiling young couple had their arms around each other, a little girl was squashed joyfully between them. My mother had always warned me not to ask Nan about them, it would only make her unhappy, so I never did. But I understood enough to know what it meant, the suddenness of their death.

I was only four when my own father died. He was already becoming a faceless stranger, the occasional unexpected visit punctuating long periods of absence. So, when his absence became a permanent thing, I barely noticed it.

But Nan had been a teenager when her parents died within weeks of each other; father in a quarry accident, mother the flu. Barely a young woman, just beginning to explore the complexities of adulthood, the loss nearly destroyed her and sent her tumbling back to the vulnerability of childhood again. The house silent, all sense of support and joy gone. It hurt, a wrenching physical hurt that set up home in her chest and wouldn't go away, wouldn't let her settle. It grew larger, a wild scratching creature gnawing behind her breastbone. She couldn't sleep or eat, or stop crying. So, one day she did the only thing she could with the pain, she tore it out. She tore her heart out of her chest then buried it in a box in the garden so it couldn't hurt her again.

A plan of sorts I suppose. But her secret wasn't her own. She was seen.

He saw her from where he'd been watching, concealed by the protection of a bramble bush which her father had been meaning to cut back for years. He saw her and after she'd left, tears and snot dripping from her chin, he dug it back up.

The box, he discarded, but he kept the heart safe in his mouth, cradled by his tongue, and when he knocked at her door the following week, he returned her heart with a kiss.

He had the reddest hair, she said. It stood up in thick tufts and wouldn't smooth down no matter how hard she tried, and amber coloured eyes that glinted when he smiled and when he was sad. She'd never seen eyes like that before, or since. But it was his kiss that caught her. When he kissed her, she thought the world would end from the joy of it. His sharp teeth would nip at her lips until she gave way completely. It became a game, a game she was always happy to lose.

It's hard to know what to say to a story like that. It's all my Nanna's life was being reduced to, a tumble of stories, of half-truths and half-remembered fictions. But they were what kept her going, and she was so very, very certain.

She showed me the scar, which of course I'd already seen, every time I bathed her. The pale pink line curved over and round her left empty breast then jagged down the middle of her chest. It stopped at the base of her ribcage in a punctuation point of knotted skin. I didn't try to remind her about the operation she'd had as a girl, when she had come so close to death. But then, that was another story she'd told me.

Because he'd returned it, her red-headed man, her heart was now his, she said. She promised him always. But despite her promises, still she lost him.

One day he failed to arrive at her door. The next day the same, and the next. She didn't know what to do, she couldn't believe he would have left her like that. She waited, days, weeks, jumping at every sound from the street, the rattle of the letterbox, keeping watch from the windows, as the pain began in her chest again.

The first time she spotted the fox in her garden, she knew, she said. And when, one morning, she found the fox sitting at her back door, as if waiting for her to open it and invite him in, what could she do? It was the eyes, you see, the same as his.

She didn't care at first, she was just so grateful that he'd returned. But the ache in her chest wouldn't go away, and she missed the strength of his arms and his kiss, and the words he used to whisper to her at night. The nip of his teeth frightened her now. All there was left to hold on to was the warmth of his fur and the shine of his amber eyes. And she was young still, foolish maybe. It grew lonely loving a fox.

And then he turned up, selling insurance. My Grandad, with his clever smile and the promise of stability.

"Turned my head. Why? Silly girl …"

There was no honeymoon, no few nights away somewhere romantic. He said they should save the money for the future. But their wedding night, at the house, was not a success. A fox screamed all night in the garden.

It was his, she said, only ever his. I promised and I let him down.

Her heart went back in a box that night.

*

Time runs out. We can make all the plans that we like, but time rarely works to the same schedule. It will always take us by surprise and leave us floundering and regretful if we are not careful.

I found the tin a day too late. She wasn't able to see it. But I had promised her. I'd held her hand with its brittle, broken nails and kissed the soft, soft down on her head and had promised her. Though I don't know if she heard me.

A week after her funeral I placed the tin in the hole she'd made, in the shade of the plum tree. I wasn't sure but it had seemed the right thing to do. I covered it over with soil, pressed the surface flat, then sat on the lawn and waited.

He came in late afternoon, as the sun cast long shadows across the grass and a chill began pulling gooseflesh from my bare arms. The sunlight caught on that orange fur again and I felt the world around me shift back to my childhood, with the smell of my Nan's kitchen and the taste of lemon squash.

My mother would have said it couldn't possibly be the same one, not after all these years. But though his muzzle was a little grizzled and his tail greyer than I remembered, he had the same crooked ear with its missing tip. And if a woman could love a man who was a fox, then surely anything was possible.

We stared at each other for a minute or two, his amber eyes unflinching, then he dropped his head and sniffed the fresh earth beneath the tree. He stood for a while, head and tail held low before curling himself to the ground over Nan's gift.

I left him there. Privacy was the last thing I could offer the both of them.

Blight of Spring

Demian Lamont

☙

I picked up Sienna's call at noon exactly. She had been calling since midnight, as she used to. My breath stopped, my chest sunk as if it was hers – not Sienna's, of course; no, she was steady. She went on to describe the whole thing in perfect calmness, with no dash of regret nor guilt nor pity; no word of condolence, no platitude. Stern. She spoke of a strange feeling at the threshold which kept her from entering the cave while Gin descended. Gin went down the fastest, smiling, "pining for the ragged depth," as Sienna put it, as if telling a story around the hearth in monotone – why would she say it like that? Then she recounted her anxiety-ridden waiting – a long waiting, longer waiting – and the violent shake of land, sharp, short and sudden; the cave roaring, collapsing; the whole underground labyrinth crackling below her body like if the planet's soul had broken asunder. A rescue team was working as we spoke, toiling to open the mouth of the endless beast that had taken Ginevra. It was not cruelty that I heard on her voice, but a soft stern cadence of soothing clarity: a somewhat sun-glimpse warmth that I'll never forgive. Like me, she knew that Gin was now of that fresh darkness. How could she then be so level, like any other day?

I was like that for weeks – it felt like years, like forever: levelled, like Sienna's voice, just without the warmth. I would lose myself for hours watching Gin's long garden growing through the windows. I was sure I would find her sooner or later crossing by the shrubs, playing with the rose's thorns, dancing at the farthest elms. Charming. I felt confused and startled

Blight of Spring

whenever someone spoke about her absence, or alluded to their grief or, worse, to mine, or discussed what arrangements should be made in *this sort of situation*, as if she was not about to be right back, about to appear walking downstairs, fair and brilliant, to meet with us.

Now, after almost six weeks have passed, I stand at the edge of Gin's garden, of summer, and of myself.

We will never have her soft figure to lay down. Her name will weather away through the seasons carved on an empty grave. And could her parents, her brother and friends – could they really let fall their soundless blessings, rain their muffled pains on there? And if I rage? If I rage, can I bring her from that foreign, shut-tight mouth back to breath, back again to here? What prayer or spell – blood to draw – what soul – ? What contraption to bend nature, wound the fates – ?

Her garden is infinite before me.

*

There is a rabbit. It takes the fruits, bounces about, digs. I see it sometimes close by, sometimes afar; it comes and goes. I cannot set foot in that place anymore; I just spy the garden's dreary spawn for a few instants from our bed or from the living room every so often by slitting open a curtain. Right now, however, I observe it. It keeps growing as I stare – slow, churning growth – a broadening greenery sparkled with flower-gems, keeps birthing its fruits under that mellow sun. Enraptured in itself, the most beautiful thing. It mocks me. Glittering husk. Full of nothing. Leaves and nothing. Wood and ground and nothing.

But there's a rabbit.

It looks at me plainly, then it bounces away! White as a ghost, in broad daylight, it disappears. I don't know where it came from, nor why. It keeps a prudent distance from the house. It's the only living thing I've seen in weeks, save for delivery people, late at night. I don't turn the lights on, or answer the phone anymore. I'm a silence and tarry so through the day. I drag it. I carry it. I try stifling this drying rage. It is sometimes the reflex of clutching my hand or my jaw at a flash of memory, a vision or a smell; or a long frown at nothing or an aslant stare at a shadow on a wall that hushes thought. The rabbit pauses to glance back again, its left ear trembles, quiet behind one of its fresh mounds, white as the dress she was wearing then. Sienna's was white too, that evening they left for Kentucky; she was the one that came up with the idea. In any case, Gin didn't need to be convinced, she would have done it all by herself if she had to. But it was Sienna.

How could Gin, vibrant and day-like as she was – she, who fancied a self-portrait in the form of a dream garden and bewitched all affections and all kindnesses around her every breath – how could she have such an urge for those barren pits? Sienna, on the other hand, with her rare sense of joking stillness, those grave, absorbing eyes and her calm voice, and that fierce subtleness of movement and expression – from her it always made sense. Yet she stayed off. Yet it is her calling right now. The phone's ring makes the rabbit stop its nibbling and turn to me once more, staring in expectation. White stare. As her smile. As the wait. As a death. Then it bounces through some brush and goes down its hole. Down it goes. The phone rings.

*

Dreams are now of scalding honey, heavy and firm along the path; a confusing amber fever. Their path is all path, and poisons each with gold. All of them end within. An intense repetition in disguise; morphing contours that blend into each other all the more with each passing sleep.

I have seen her at the end of a long street, surrendering herself to a night of black stars in sheer gladness, but I am a tree left on the sidewalk and cannot speak her name.

I have seen myself winding on the inside: neither beginning nor end, a thing without a centre, a place around itself without name nor location.

I have seen her stopped in motion, the first of three echoing halts, like if she had ere crafted that nether space herself to use it as her maw, steady, since a time well beyond time.

I sleep most of the time, but I don't want these dreams: as much as I forget awake, their heat scars my thoughts.

*

Over this unyielding pavement, all things brim with voice and movement; they inhale, expand and say I've been part of it before. Now I cannot feel myself blend with its rhythms. This world forward. As I turn around the corners, I feel as if bound to my dim bedroom; every crossing of the road is going up the living room stairs; walking down the avenue is walking down one of those halls; and all the rooms, the stairs, the halls, dry walls of that circular house lead ever away into her radiant grove. So, even if I scape the architecture, I carry within that self-wrapping mechanism as I would bone, breath, feeling. Yet, it is Sienna whom I remember at the entrance of the mall and, all of a sudden, I feel grounded by her ease. I can see distinctly every person, every light, all reflections on the gleaming floors. "It is all tightly woven, like a good scarf." I took a trolley and followed her as if I didn't know where she was going, but she pathed the place the same way every time. "It is because it's always the same place, although Ginny may tell you otherwise," but I was too busy at the flowers of her shirt to reply. "I always do the same track because I enjoy it! I, you see, have perfected the mall, like one day so will the city and all the roads. I know the best routes and their twists, and the mysteries hidden along the way: at what time you can get the very best bread, and which trolleys work properly, unlike the one you're hauling around." My trolley wants to go left. "You would just go about. The only thing that you care perfecting is the circles you make around your bedroom," she continued with a controlled smile while holding a bundle of rosemary with the care one would a weapon.

"It just seems a little obsessive," although I only half meant it; I actually liked it.

"No, don't be silly. Obsession haunts and threats. What I do is build myself a proper road and walk it. I walk, learn my walking and walk better.

"The planet around the sun: *that* is an obsession, constantly falling into that monstrous thing of fire, knowing that deviating its fall would just kill it the fastest. I can change this route at a whim." So with the trolley half full of scented candles, nuts and spices we turned right, as I struggle, towards the fruit instead of the meat. "Keep up."

"Well, it doesn't matter if I were to get us all the fruit in here; it wouldn't last two days in that house, you can't help it."

"*Well*, take what you will then."

I consider the apples, the pears, the pictures, the oranges, and after careful study, I take only a cluster of grapes that reminds me of a heart, but she just as readily had piled up an assortment of fruit, far enough from the bundles of spices to not crush them.

Past the longest hall, we get the freshest bread, which would be usually the last item, and downstairs – I, fighting the disposition of the trolley – we collect nuts, dried berries and some essentials.

"She would be annoyed, you know," without looking at me.

"Why? How so?"

"She likes my route. Well, with her is not quite the same one. Plus, she doesn't follow me through the whole of it like some lost puppy," now turning to me with piercing eyes.

"Ah, so you would go try clothes for her."

"In here? No, never."

"Go stare at the pianos, perhaps."

"The keyboards, yes, and would play about twenty seconds of a something for her."

"Of what song?"

"Of a song."

"But they're often unplugged."

"Even so."

"And through the gardening section at the end."

"That sounds terribly intimate." She put wine from the cupboard in the trolley and headed for olive oil.

"And you would."

"Would it get to you, if she were to tell me about what brand of weeders she likes better? Oh! *Well*, look at the mess you've made again!"

The trolley had finally beaten my grip leftwards to crash against and throw a couple of oil bottles off a bookshelf. I give her a vexed glance, but she is already stealing away, so I hurry past the wreck and out the room to meet her at the checkout. She seemed awfully pleased with herself and smiled at me as if in jest, but with an expression slightly too sincere for my liking.

"Want a short walk in the park? It's lovely today. We'll just leave this in the trunk," she took the chianti first to the band.

"Gin – "

"Likes us spending time together."

I take a moment to think, to think, to think of thinking about what am I doing as I pile up the groceries on the counter, like reading over and over the same line of dialogue.

"Well, she will be there anyway," she says while I pay.

"What? In the park?" I take the grapes and we head out.

"'In the park?'" he says…

"You're gonna bury those."

The door of the mall opens directly into grass and marigolds. As I walk forward, people lessen until I see none around. I kneel and claw into the fresh earth, digging the hole where I put the grapes after taking one for myself. I cover the rest up. Only the rabbit watches me in wonder a few steps away while I put the one piece of fruit in my mouth. I go back in, lay down on the couch, eyes closed. As it starts raining, I can feel a hot grasp around my bare feet that travels through my whole frame, a beating coming from the turf of the grove that feels like black roots running throughout its soil, entwining, spreading. That pulse ends in myself and, as if it were myself, it lets me touch the twines of every brush, the cold droplets being drunk by the fresh ground, the white rabbit outdoors, which shakes with the pulse too. It is digging its holes, the rabbit now: it breathes and digs deep on, digging a net of veins, expands, digging under the very skin of Ginevra. Digging caves.

*

It beats, and paints within me the end of every branch.

It beats, and I can feel the empty house in full.

It beats, and the rabbit and every hidden crawler creep through me.

It beats. It beats. It beats. It beats.

It scares me, but I gradually get used to it.

*

Three weeks ago, her brother was here. He came to check on me and talked about work and his last couple of travels. He was, as ever, very gentle, and helped me to clean the place a little before we took a seat. The music started playing without me even noticing; when I regained awareness from deep thought, the gramophone had conquered the whole house.

His expressions, the light in his eyes, his gestures while speaking seemed at times an eerie repetition of his twin's, so I tried to not look at him much. That, too, might be the reason he didn't speak of her, besides a slight allusion, a yellow-veiled suggestion, as if her direct mention could only be redundant. They, however, were barely alike in character, and, despite my first sentiment when he showed up being a mix of black whirls in the mind, his presence soon came to feel as one of a charming stranger. It soothed me sincerely. It turned the space itself into another and did the same to me: it turned me into a resemblance of myself, same person of different meaning, a *rhyme of I* of sorts.

"Her sister was a poet," he said; "… and mom planned the whole wedding," he said; "… so I've been learning Italian," he said and said, and went on like that for long hours. I nodded and smiled and talked back little during the whole coversation, if one could call it that, but it filled me with pleasure just to listen. I could almost ignore its digging through, outside; the beat that brought to me the texture of the barks and the earth and the multiple, constantly expanding burrows. There could not be a time better than that one, which we spent between drinks and light anew, between our idle chats and merry little care. I thought myself now rescued from an eternity soon to be forgotten.

The lovely warmth of lights would go then mingle with that of breaths less laden with word's meanings, and lights would twist in turn into novel, trembling forms.

Later, I walked him to his car.

Once he was gone, I noticed the leaves had started to fall along the street, matching their reddish colours to the twilight's. As I walked back into the house, I could feel coming from there inside the burning beatings through the burrows.

*

I go out often. The strict, warm browns of autumn make the outlines of my stream of thought distinct; I can think with precision and direction, and the last months appear to be almost a flickering reverie. I crush the leaves under my shoes and have no sudden beating through my body telling of their crisp edges; not when I'm outside, afar. I only feel the wind against my face and the pull of the yellow scarf weaving at the wind. These last days, I have sought the company of a few old acquaintances; I've walked around the park's lake to watch the ducks and gone out with new people to new places. Sienna wouldn't answer my calls, so I stopped trying. It makes but little difference. Now I can see the world as it is again, its surface and its shapes as they are meant to be perceived. The solid streets hold me upright. I dally at a coffee or a bar and try not to think of the work piling up at the house to steal my nights away, nor of the house itself. I try to think only of that which is apparent.

Night closes round every time to always lead me back there.

I close the door behind me and take my coat off, hang the keys and feel the beating caves calling me firmly, the darkness through them shaped like writhing serpents. Every night I come back to find her forest of evergreen blight tolling, a dizzying emerald hidden here in the middle of this autumn, endless wound, connected to all. Itself, slowly, irrevocably, all. All earth, gravel, clay; all the depths and dreadful heights; all gardens, canyons, caverns and ravines and flesh of fruit and mountain and beast; all of them the same creature, waiting for me right there, with this pulse as its centre, unyielding.

Tonight, however, it will end. I have felt the day coming for a long time, despair accumulating gradually. I've known it'd be today since I woke up; even when I fled in anxious hurry, I had decided already the destiny of my enemy. I take a deep breath as I head for the shed and take the shears. I walk, no hesitation, into the garden, so steadily that I can't help but feeling proud and noble. I face it tall and poised. The raw ground beats stronger as I walk in, stronger as I move close to dead center. I try to keep my rhythm, but it rattles my bones. Lungs. Skull. Pangs. Throbs. I run against the closest bush and wreck it. The next one falls into rubble just as quickly. I make my way as fire, severing every flower and fruit, chopping through them, leaving behind but rubbish, coarse branches with mutilated leaves. I slash at trunks and scream against their gashed bark, and kick and stab the lawn haphazardly to pierce by chance its tolling heart, puncture its veins and slay the ceaseless rabbit.

At length, as I have ravished ages of invincible green, and my body is exhausted and the shears ruined and my hands battered and sore, I look behind me to contemplate victory. I see the house no more. I look harder, left and right, round and front.

There is only forest, infinite before me.

*

The moon has waxed and waned so many times. I have endured rains, cold, sleepless walks, relentless heat, wounds, thirst, and hunger. The forest still sustains me. I did all but completely consume it in despair. It stands. It gives. It takes. It grows. Its every grain of earth beats within my heart. I can sense at my bare feet the shapes of every mountain; I know the form of every stone, tree, mushroom; every precise blade of grass as if they were my fingers. I know the worm, the owl, the fox, the rabbit, the spider. Every hunt. Every dryad. I'm the whole wound at once and walk on carrying that weight.

Deep into farther grounds, I feel the trees abate and the palpitations muddle by a nest of strange movements: earthly poisoned rivers of unceasing flesh.

*

The days grow colder and ashen. No fire can withstand. There is no small animal to take, only petty fruits and insects abate hunger. I hold the gilded scarf tight around me. Voices of bears rush through me from afar. I know I will pass by them as our eyes briefly meet. This path only goes forward. Green. Red. Golden.

*

You see me now, but the forms beating through me here are blurry. The earth moves as if it were water, its insides brimming with serpents like a current. They writhe under my steps and spire towards the center of it all.

The winds are void of all heat and cut right past me. The trees grow pale as I do, and the leaves dwindle.

*

You see me. Among the biting storm, the last of dreary trees gives way to nothing, and all the guidance of the writhing snakes goes at once quiet. The entrance glares at me now, breathing darkness forward. It is the eye, the mouth, the wound, the artery, the call.

As my silhouette is extinguished, engulfed by the great night of its interior, any suspicion of an outside flees away. The crude rock without forms, the sharp eclipse of things, the bottomless invisible – it swallows.

*

There is barely anything left of me, torn further by the jagged nothingness at every step. Endless corridors and recesses, accidents, and sudden falls; narrow tunnels and titanic galleries of echo: something of me is left at each and every. There is only *need* to drive me onwards.

*

Above, eons of this body's blood feed the walls of the temple, feeds all the things which appeared through dirt and mud, for this temple has no end and no beginning, and births whatever was and is and will be. Life and Death are its mute song, its transparent structure. If there is any material left of me, it is the seed which will fall at the center of this nowhere, and from which every form will take its being.

*

I see you. Forward, a piece of wall that is distinguished by the eye, which can barely stay half open against a mere reflection of a light source. A turn. And at the embrace of warm, it opens up complete to me: a fierce sun shines its beauty tall and center of a titanic egg-shaped chamber covered fully by manifold foliage whose forms and patterns change wherever I set my weak eyes upon them, yet they unite into one perfect composition.

I rain over the Garden of Ginevra.

*

As I steadily appear, lying on the wet grass, the first thread of sunshine pours right on my skin. I stand up slowly, breathe in and observe the house, that ancient place that was once more than dreams of deep thought. It is as I remember. Before my taking shelter within it and making peace with the despair it once encompassed, I look back at the Garden, broken by my old cuts and struck with weary winter. I pause to acknowledge her with care: the bare branches, still covered by patches of melting snow, glitter under the sun's sigh.

As spring approaches round, her flowers will speak their myths and secrets once again. Her voice echoes through me still the forms and textures all around. We now both know the words.

The Mountains like Waves

Trish Marriott

ଔ

The road through the High Atlas reaches 1500m above sea level, although the summit is much higher. The Anti Atlas mountains to the south are some of the oldest visible geology in the world. The collision of the African and Iberian tectonic plates way back in pre-history resulted in vertical plate movement of up to 11 km in this area. From the road the mountains look like waves in the distance.

By road it is 448km from Marrakesh to M'Hamid. The regular bus service takes 7-10 hours, but us tourists take 2 days as we stop all the time for food, shopping, and photo ops. And to buy watermelons.

The road south: Ouarzazate to M'Hamid

Multi-coloured hibiscus spills over walls, red, orange, white, purple, billowing
    splitting slabs of slate ready to spill over the side of the mountain.
    Huge boulders, poised to fall from the very top and roll. All the way down
    the Anti-Atlas are older than the High Atlas, so much older. You can see the layers of the seabed, all tipped up by tectonic movement so the mountains look like waves.
    The greeny shale spills down over the red rock. From a distance you can't tell which is doing what. Is the red spilling down in great fans across the slopes or is it the green?

The mountains have vertical stripes here, red, green, white salt, occasional yellow in rainbow stripes

painted rock faces.

Softer rock spilling away from the harder rock leaving cones and plateaus

the great solar array glints in the far distance. There are clouds above it, almost as if it generates its own weather.

Across the plain from Ouarzazate and down, down into the valley to the oasis of Fint. Lush and green by the river, grapevines tumbling over fencing. The egrets flying over the oasis at dusk, snakes fishing, frogs calling, the blessing of water and green growth, a balm for the soul.

And back up we go, to the sea of stones, and the mountains, always the mountains in the distance, rolling, rolling, rolling like waves.

The palmeries grow closer.

As we leave the great mountains of the High Atlas behind, the waves in the ground start to swell. The seabed sticks out in places like the backbone of some huge, long dead sea creature.

At Zagora, the old mountains start to rise

rise and fall again in horizontal stripes,

pink rock

deep gorges,

granite pillars huddled together at the peaks like lines of broken tombstones.

South of Zagora the green begins to fade away.

The stone gives way to sand gradually, the acacias following invisible lines. The lines of the seabed move from diagonal to vertical, sticking upside-on briefly then disappearing into the sand again.

At Agdez it really begins.

The mountaintops in the distance are green streaked with white, haze shrouded

the mountain of glass.

The Salt Road from Telouet to Mali.

The mountains break away and the valley opens up

palm trees line the riverbed.

Past Tamegrout the great bowl of the mountains circles the plain where the First Dune lies by the Observatory. On one side the stripes in the mountains lie horizontal, on the other, tipped, breaking like waves.

The sand begins as we approach the gap, but the road turns away heading south

a huge dust devil marches along the road with us, finally fading over a football pitch marked out in stones.

The lines of the seabed in the distance, getting wider and stronger. At the tops where they are weathered, a look of the great menhirs and sarsens of the north.

The road turns again as we cross the river once more and start to climb through the pass.

The rocks above line up like tombstones, weathered, splitting, teeth, caves in between

where they have fallen away they are pink on the inside, weathered grey on the outside.

The weathered stones watch, lower it seems, but we are at the top, almost beside them now. As we clear the pass another plain opens up below.

The mountains round it are so far away, but so very present. Surrounding us, like a protective circle. Breaking like waves in the distance

The colours of the ground change from brown and dark grey to lighter sandy colours, but always the sagey greens, acacia trees and palms.

The palmeries begin again, we see the tagine-shaped mountain far, far ahead, Ben Sulaiman. So much haze, is this the moisture in the air still from all the rain in spring?

The new apartments at Tagounite with their crenelated edges. The unmade road through the town.

36 km to Algeria the sign says. We aren't going that way.

As we pass Ben Sulaiman the yellow warning signs line the road. Beware desert.

We can see dunes now, and far, far away the water tower at M'Hamid

the mountains behind us rise like waves.

The stones finally give way to sand. Peppered with acacias and tamarisk the dunes grow. Palms grow around the villages along the road as it winds through the oases of the South.

The kingdom of Tidri where the Jews settled

and the mountains like waves in the distance.

It is peaceful as the light dims

the moon has already risen high, veiled by clouds. The stars peek out

as we look north, the mountains like waves in the distance.

Always.

Rolling, rolling, like waves.

The road north: M'Hamid to Ouarzazate

We leave the desert behind us and drive North towards the mountains,

the kingdom of Tidri where the Jews settled,

and the mountains like waves in the distance.

The stripes in the rocks of the mountains where the road cuts around

past Ben Sulaiman, the sand collects against the foothills of the mountain and encroaches the oasis, thwarted only by cassia and tamarisk.

The sea of stones begins, the mountains surrounding us, a protective circle.

Far away the water towers of tiny villages stand against the mountains. The road curves gently, slowly around and we drive past them. Water towers and solar powered well heads standing alone in a sea of stones.

Flat, spread out for miles. A gentle rise, another well head, the power lines march alongside the road.

The mountains once so far away are closer now,

the green rock spills away from the granite in fans.

Camels.

Acacia.

The hills surround the road here,

a well head with no tower stands alone by the side of the road as we climb to the pass. The stones are rocks and much bigger and closer now. Bigger than cars, smaller than buses

we head down past splitting granite teeth.

A steeper descent into the next valley

steeper again, switchbacks starting.

The mountain towers above us as we head down into the valley opened up at our feet, a great flat plain surrounded by mountains, rolling like waves.

Acacia.

And stones.

The palmeries in the distance surrounded by haze

and the mountains, so very far away, but ever present, like waves in the distance.

The observatory and the first dune. On one side of the wide valley the seabed in the mountains is horizontal, on the other breaking like waves and the palmeries in between the sand is almost gone now.

A stony football pitch outside the town,

the sea of stones and the mountains growing closer.

Dust devils.

Acacia scrub defying the scorching sun.

Approaching Agdez the mountains are green and grey streaked with white. This is part of the old salt road to Timboctou.

Climbing again, slowly, black-tipped hills and the waves of the mountains beyond

The valley below seems so far away, yet we were there only a few minutes ago.

The grey green shale washed away by snowmelt to show the darker rocks below.

The colours of the rocks revealed by the building of the new road

zig-zag up, across the top then down.

The grasses return almost without notice

watermelon lorries leave Zagora.

The sun lowers in the sky and people start to move about.

The motor engineers spill their workshops over the approaches,

the great palmeries on our right, and to the West the lowering sun over the ever-present mountains, rolling

we climb.

More green on the hillsides.

Terracotta walls – paint now, not the raw terracotta bricks made from the red earth beneath.

The distant mountains are now suddenly closer. No gentle rises here, straight up from the plain

the road slices round the sides, granite cliffs on one side, palms on the other. The river between the road and the palmeries.

The Mountains like Waves

Still we climb.
The waves begin to roll, misty in the overcast.
Raw sandstone spills from between the granite plates,
Green fans spilling away, and we descend.

As the sun lowers, the temperature drops. The shops open, people gather at the cafes, beds and mattresses make an appearance outside the roadside shops. The watermelon lorries are parked up now ready to move on once darkness falls. No driving in twilight on these winding roads.

The road winds, heading for the pass

Villages are more numerous, the new, grey buildings by the road while a mud brick ksar moulders on a hilltop, watching

modern buildings, window bars different in each one watch the road

And always the mountains
Behind
And ahead
And either side, rolling, breaking, like waves
We climb
we approach the pass
the mountains are green.

We cross the pass and start to descend into the palms by the river.

The river is full enough to flow, but not spilling out onto the flood plain below the road,

we can see the clouds forming round the solar array, is it really raining over there?

The mountains are more present – immediate, but still so very far away

between us and them, hills like coal heaps with the road winding through them following the river north.

You can still see the waves, rolling.

The Golden Hour is gone, the sun will set soon, 1 hour to Ouazarzate.

The green is new growth,

the rains in spring were too late to save all the palms of the South, but the mountains here are green.

We climb. Spillways litter the mountainside

we climb, and climb

as we near the top, then turn away, the great stone teeth of the mountains above us and the road spread across the valley below,

and in the distance, the mountains like waves.

Ouarzazate – Marrakesh. An early start to a long day

Cassia trees. Long stems, tiny leaves, and the heady aroma of the yellowy-orangey flowers

the crumbling ksars on the hilltops.

The cats waiting by the butcher's counter till he invites them up,

children on their way to school. Greens for the animals being carried in great bundles on women's backs, on mopeds, in barrows.

The ever-present moto workshops smell of grease and 2-stroke,

a gazebo in the middle of the roundabout provides shade for the traffic officers.

Incongruous cypress trees line the golf course. So far south?

A stork's nest on top of the mosque tower.

bamboo plantations.

Dune buggies for sale (or rent) (are we singing yet?)

The road rises and falls

the mountains are closer now, rising and falling away

We are climbing now, the road winds round hills peppered with stones and scrub,

another plain ahead, and in the distance, the mountains, like waves.

The seabed breaks through as we wind up the mountains again, higher, and higher,

Ouazarzate is so very very far below.

We drift down the mountainside again, villages far away on the valley floor, red brick, grey plaster, terracotta and cream paint

and ahead the Atlas in the mist so very far away.

On our right, the mountains break, like waves.

You notice the green more as you return from the desert. A sea of grasses and crop plots,

trees of all kinds line the waterways

and the mountains, towering over the villages, and yet, in the distance, more. Higher, darker. The High Atlas.

Olive trees. Red brick buildings tumble down the hillside as the green rock pours over the red earth.

In the far distance there is still snow on the highest peaks,

Caves in the hills. So steep, so high, but the Atlas still higher, beyond

a village perched on a cliff face,

a diversion round a bit of partly-finished new road.

The school buses ready to collect the children and return them to their homes. Their day starts early and finishes by noon.

My eyes can see the snow on the Atlas Mountains, here in the red valley it is dry and hot,

a broken watermelon lies alone by the side of the road.

We are much higher now, my ears pop as we enter the Atlas.

The green rhassoul, the red mud, a tiny set of terraces planted with crops. The road winds through the mountain

villages climbing, climbing, climbing
> blankets laid on the hillside along the river to dry.
> A line of granite far, far above
> green and grey and red in stripes.

The snowy stripes are closer now, but still far away. An hour ago, they were barely visible.
> Roadbuilding equipment lies unattended in the heat of midday while the workers rest,
> the grasses hold the hillsides in place.

We are in the Atlas now, but the High Atlas still tower above us breaking like waves and falling away
> Aloes line the road as we climb again
> we enter the High Atlas,

The road crews are back, wrapped up against the sun. Its cooler at this altitude, but the sun is still strong.
> More terraced crops, every bit of space used,
> snow markers line the edge of the road while the mountains still tower above us
> we climb. Saplings march along the mountainside.
> Red, red rock, a blond goat with a long coat grazes above us,
> salt stains on the newly exposed rockfaces, white on grey striped rock: red, grey, green, white.
> Above us grass and gorse glue the surface together
> my ears pop some more,
> we reach the top. Well, as high as the road can go. Col Tichka is over 2000m above sea level, but the road lies 500m below that. The Berber name is Tizi n'Tichka – Difficult Mountain pasture.
> Stripey rocks and quartz veins. This is where the minerals are, amethyst, selenite, ammonites
> the blue blue sky, the fluffy clouds.

The switchbacks in the road lined with snow markers by the drops reveal the spillways under the road ahead.

The snow above still clinging to the higher valleys,
we are so very high, but they are higher still,
the stripey shale and slate melts by the roadside.
108km to Marrakesh.
Ears popping again.
So green at the bottom of the valleys so far below,
steep mountainsides green with scrub and new olive trees
The rock. High, steep.
Terraces no wider than a path lining the mountain with growing crops,
the sideways slant of the rockface, angles changing round each bend in the road
Sharp edges, sudden stops. Green mud turning to shale,
too close to see the waves now, are they still there?
Burnt orange rock bleeding down to the road,
gullys cutting down the mountainside.
The river below
the old road swoops round a curve that the new road cuts right through.
The mountains tower above us.
Olive trees, and an entirely unexpected palm. Roses in bloom. Silver birch trees line the river
cream, grey, red where the road cuts through and a stilted aqueduct running alongside.
The new homes here are painted a deep red with cream edges, the older ones now a faded terracotta. They make the plaster from the red earth.
In time all the new bright cuttings will fade.
The engine labours as we climb,
already the mud exposed by the roadworks in the last few years have deep grooves cut by snowmelt.
Cratered rocks form a waterfall, empty now, but in early

spring this will be overflowing.

Red scrub on the red rocks. Alpine plants taking root in cracks in the exposed surfaces,

solid bands of colour.

Pines grow here, this is the wooded mountain. A pine plantation experiment in the European style. An incongruous forester's cottage with its pitched roof, so very different from the flat roofs favoured here.

Exposed roots like fingers gripping.

In the pine forest, high in the mountains,

so very green here with red or cream rock in the exposed places.

Rain patters across the road evaporating immediately.

The diggers perch high above us as we go through the roadworks,

terraces stripe the mountainside ahead.

Geraniums spill over a wall,

tiny patches of barley, no bigger than my patio,

rocks litter the slopes ready to fall.

Olive trees and tiny gardens.

We are through the High Atlas now, but ahead the mountains remain, still breaking

like waves.

Like waves breaking.

They remember the sea.

The red, red soil is cultivated. Small farms, fields delineated by trails of rock on the slopes

Its cooler, relatively. The middle schoolers are out now. Young men gather at the cafes, and someone straps a double bed base to the roof of a tiny car.

The breaking mountains are punctuated by olive trees.

There it is again – written in white-painted rock – Allah,

al Watah, al Malik – God, Country, King – high on the mountainside among the olives. We see this everywhere the king has travelled. His people love him.

I fell asleep. I always sleep through this part of the journey.

When I wake, we are on the plains, heading for Marrakesh. No mountains ahead, they are behind us now

Rolling
Breaking
Like waves.

Tiny White Flowers

Ivy Senna

ଓ

You terrified me, the first time we met. Your leaves were not green, but blackened and brittle, dead before they even fell. Your branches were twisted and gnarled, like crooked fingers clutching at the sky. They writhe like slithering snakes, and I could tell that the bark was not merely bark but also bone – flesh and bone, thrumming alive just beneath the surface. You looked down at me with glowing green eyes, the color a sickly green as if a disease had taken root in them. I heard a low rumble and realised that it was your voice: deep and resounding and rasping, like dry leaves crushed underfoot or the scraping of flintstones. Bereft of words, I swallowed and held my breath. With haunted eyes, I stared upwards at your looming figure.

"You shouldn't be here," you said, coldly.

I only nodded in response and made my way to leave.

Except, I had nowhere to go. I wasn't lost, but on the run.

I glanced back at you. The moonlight that shone down upon your knotted branches cast a silver glow upon its rough surface. Amidst the stark contrast of light and dark, the silhouette of thorns jutted out from the branches like the sharpened claws of some wild beast. You must've sensed my hesitation, for something in you softened. For a moment, the brief time between one heartbeat and the next, even those jagged thorns seemed gentle.

I knew then that you had relented – that you'd allowed me to stay.

"One night," I whispered, pleading. "And then I'll be gone."

It seemed I was a liar.

I didn't mean to lie, it was just that – somehow, yoked by the hunger of my throbbing heart – one night turned into two, and two nights turned into ten. Before we both realised it, I had spent a month in this time-abandoned wilderness.

You like it too, don't you? I wanted to ask. *Does my company bring you joy?*

All I knew then was that I had fallen in love with your star-shaped flowers, the delicate petals unfurling – white like snowdrops, pale before the dark and thorny branches. I rested my head against your bark and you angled your sharpness away. One prick and I would be doomed: a sleeping beauty pricking her finger against the spindle, never to awaken. Still, I was unafraid. I breathed in your dew-drenched scent and sighed. I closed my eyes: I could die now and be at peace, so long as you were by my side.

I dreamed of fertile earth, bloodied and damp, dew-soaked and rain wet. I dreamed of roots that hungered for blood, wanting for rot and decomposition. You feasted on cadavers and carcasses alike, only to transform them into new life– into flowers, into fruits, into leaves. You feasted on my shame too. That which others turn their heads away from, you embrace. Nothing in me was too dirty or rotten for you. After all, were you not a seed, born from dirt? Were there not worms churning beneath your earth?

Am I not a child of earth and starry heaven?

Your comforting presence almost erased the memory of why I was on the run in the first place. I had almost forgotten why I was hounded out and hunted like an animal. Still, I sometimes hear their words like knives in my mind: dissecting me, dismembering me. No tears would come, yet my cheeks would flush. No crime that I had committed justified this mutilation, this desecration of the self. In my nightmares I heard your voice, your words and ancient wisdom grounding me to reality.

I am not a virgin to be sacrificed to a cruel and sadistic god.
I am not the sewer silt that a serpent would breed upon.
I am not filled with putrid sludge; if I open my mouth, no fetid slime would spill out.

In the silence of the woods, you taught me how to sing. My words were no longer whispers, but cries and lamentations and the keening wail of grief. I mourned for the girl I was and the woman I could have been. I mourned for the butterflies I failed to chase and the flower fields I never played in. To my surprise, you wept with me too. Your sap, like tears, flowed down the length of your trunk in solemn rivulets. The wine-dark juice seeped from your sloe, infusing the air with its sorrowful fragrance.

For the first time, I felt like I was seen: my grief reflected in your grief, my tears reflected in your tears.

*

Spring came and went and I stopped counting the years I spent here. Yet, time was unforgiving in its march, leaving none untouched against its ravages.

I should've known that this day would come, ever since my eyes met yours.

With every passing season, I could not help but notice the way your already fragile leaves began to take on a metallic tint. A spectral pallor haunted the leaves, casting an ethereal silver sheen upon their surfaces like a tarnished mirror. Irregular patches of silver spread across the foliage – a creeping, insidious malaise. The edges of your leaves curled ever so slightly, as if recoiling from the unseen torment that had befallen them. Your branches, once adorned with delicate blossoms, now wore a desolate crown. Flowers, once ivory white, had withered into dry husks.

I saw upon you the relentless toll of time's indifference.

"You're dying, aren't you?" I asked, even though I already knew the answer. "Is there really nothing I can do?"

You were silent, offering me no reply. Gently, I plucked one of your sickened leaves and placed it in my pocket.

I knew this day would come eventually – the day I am, for one reason for another, forced to return to the dreaded town I once called home. The journey back was a solemn one. The narrow streets, paved with cobblestones, reminded me of a time I longed to escape from. I could hear the whispers of disapproval, the scorn that lingered in the air. Their eyes – sharp like a scorpion's stinger – followed my every move, their piercing gaze an unwelcome reminder of the fact that I did not belong. The picturesque facades of the perfect rows of houses masked the stories of a wounded youth. Keeping my head low, I trudged forward.

The arborist's cottage was located at the opposite end of the town.

Nestled amidst a hand-grown grove of trees, the cottage stood with a timeless grace. Ivy vines, adorned with delicate blossoms, clung to its walls. The windows, much like the walls, were framed by the soft green drapery of the verdant ivy. Above the rustic stone walls of the cottage, a thatched roof crowned the dwelling like a wild, woven diadem. The thick straw – a tapestry of subtle hues, from sun-bleached gold to the deepest earthy brown – traced the tale of a craftsmanship honed by countless generations. Here and there, a stray straw or two poked out rebelliously from the otherwise orderly formation. The door of the cottage, crafted from weathered oak, bore the muted patina of countless seasons.

It was as if nothing had changed since I left.

I knocked, and the door swung open.

The arborist gasped.

"You're back!"

Before I could utter a response, I was pulled into an embrace – a warmth flooded my chest. In spite of everything, I found myself leaning into the touch. A sigh escaped my lips, nostalgia feeling like a snug blanket.

After all, the arborist was the only reason I remained sane in this place.

"I'm not staying long," I explained. "I have a favor to ask: can you fix this?"

I showed the arborist the leaf, its surface covered by a dull silver.

The arborist took the leaf in his hands, examining it with a frown.

"This is no ordinary disease," the arborist shook his head. "On the surface, it looks like *silver leaf*. A fungal infection, progressive and often fatal."

"Fatal?"

"If it was merely silver leaf I'd simply advise you to prune and burn the affected branches," the arborist continued. "But this isn't it."

"What is it then?"

"A curse."

It was as if time itself had paused. I stood there like a startled deer, eyes wide with astonishment, frozen amidst the tangled thicket of bewilderment.

"What manner of witchcraft have you gotten yourself into?" the arborist asked, his voice low. "No, don't tell me – I don't want to know. Still, if you insist, you can try pruning and burning the branches but I cannot guarantee that it will be a cure."

With my mind spinning, I thanked the arborist for his time and made my journey back into the woods.

It did not take long for me to find a suitable tool.

That cloudless night, I stood before you, trembling.

I took in a sharp breath, a blade in hand.

The pruning saw, its blade like a sickle moon, caught the moonlight with a lustrous sheen. This was not a butchery, I told myself, but a surgery. The saw was not some murder weapon, but a scalpel. I willed my hand to steady and not shake, imagining myself as some sort of surgeon: a sculptor of flesh and bone or, in this case, of bough and twig. I closed my eyes before reopening them, gathering my resolve. In that quiet, I felt your presence like a hand on my shoulder.

"Go on," you seemed to say.

I tightened my grip upon the blade's handle and began to cut.

The first cut was a hesitant whisper, the saw's teeth biting into the diseased bough, the scraping and slicing noise shattering the silence. I feel you shivering beneath my blade, an echo of pain traveling down your bark. Determined, I continued, the saw moving back and forth rhythmically. Each stroke was made with diligent precision and meticulous care. Eventually, the diseased wood gave way under my touch, the scent of fresh sap and decay mingling in the air. The diseased branches fell away with a sigh.

Bit by bit, I cut my way through each infected branch and once the process was complete, I set the prunings aflame.

There was a beauty in the way the branches burned: a funeral pyre for the fallen branches. The fire took to the wood with a lover's fervor, the bark crackling beneath the heat. Each branch, each twig, each sliver of wood that fell to the flames was a scar healed, a wound cauterized. The flames grew, consuming the wood with a ravenous brutality. The pyre continued to grow taller and taller, fumes of smoking rising in billowing columns like a ghost exorcized by the cleansing fire. It swirled into the night sky, a dark wraith against the canvas of stars, the scent of burning wood and the sweet promise of regeneration hanging heavy like a thick perfume. As the embers began to die, I watched as the last of the diseased wood turned to ash.

The fire's glow dimmed and darkness returned to the woods.

Yet, despite my efforts, your new shoots sprouted silver.

No blade nor flame could break the curse.

*

There was a story I heard in my youth of a wise woman who could charm a sickness out of a man and into a pig, or an illness out of cattle and into a dog. The same could supposedly be done for curses: a transference of the evil eye from one being onto another, for example. It was a tale spoken in hushed whispers, not to be repeated in polite society lest one wished to be accused of being a witch. With the memory of my mother's words in my mind, I set out to capture an animal – a sacrifice to bear the curse in your stead.

The first creature I found was a nightingale.

A solitary nightingale was chirping upon the bough of a cedar tree, a vessel of song with brown plumage and beady, dark eyes. My heart pounded in rhythm with the bird's melody as I reached out, hands cradling the air around it. With a quick lunge, I captured the nightingale in my grasp, lithe fingers closing around the delicate creature. I could feel the rapid flutter of its heart like a tiny drum against my palm. Its song had faltered, replaced by the frantic rustle of feathers against my skin. As I placed the songbird within a makeshift cage, the nightingale flapped its wings, a flurry of feathers and panic.

Tiny White Flowers

The songbird flitted about, a whirlwind of feathers and fear, the cage's bar clanging. I watched as it eventually settled upon the cage's perch, its chest heaving, its eyes – dark and beady – staring back at me.

Staring back at the nightingale, I made my way back to you.

I whispered the sacred words to coax the curse out of the wood and into your thorn.

Then, taking a deep breath, I fetched the songbird from its cage and pressed its chest against the thorn.

Blood dripped from the wound and the nightingale fell still, its song forever silenced. I gasped, noticing the way the silver sheen appeared to fade from your leaves. Tears pricked at my eyes when I felt the songbird growing cold, its feathers turning a metallic, silver hue upon its death. It seemed the ritual had worked– and yet, it wasn't enough. The nightingale was but a tiny creature, young and trifling. I needed a larger animal, a vessel large enough to hold all of the baleful corruption.

The second creature I found was a wild horse.

In the wild expanse of an open grass meadow, a figure of untamed elegance grazed under the cerulean sky. The equine's coat was a shimmering canvas of chestnut and cream. Powerful muscles rippled beneath its sleek hide as its mane, a cascade of sable, danced freely in the wind. I stood at the edge of the meadow; an apple clutched in my hand. The fruit, plump and red, was not just an offering, but a lure imbued with a sleep-inducing poison, a tranquilizer to put the horse into a temporary slumber.

I led the horse to where you stood and, when the moment was right, allowed the horse to take its bite. The poison took effect within minutes. The creature's legs buckled, the once powerful beast sinking onto the soft earth with a muted thud.

I breathed a sigh of relief and whispered an apology into the slumbering horse's ear.

Making my way back towards you, I recited the holy words once again. Careful not to injure myself, I plucked a thorn and raised it before the horse like a ceremonial knife –

And plunged.

Like previously, the silver curse ebbed away from your leaves and the equine corpse became tainted with that same mercurial tint, the curse being successfully transferred.

And yet, it was not enough. Somehow, even the body of a strong and healthy wild horse was not enough.

"Don't do it," you whispered to me. I feel a gnarled branch of yours curling against my wrists, tugging at me, pleading me to reconsider

Gently, I shook my head and planted a kiss upon your bough.

I knew exactly what I had to do.

That night, I dressed myself in white, wearing my late mother's old wedding gown – the one possession I refuse to discard or sell. I once imagined myself as a bride, walking down the aisle with flower petals strewn to herald my footsteps. The music, oh, how it would have filled the air! The strumming of the lute, the lilting notes of the violin and the sound of laughter echoing throughout a gilded hall. The teenage me had wanted honey cakes for my wedding. The air would be sweetened with honey, perfumed by the scent of roses.

I certainly was a hopeful child.

The sky was starless that night. Smiling, I incanted those arcane words for a third time, then pricked my finger upon your thorn. A tiny droplet of blood welled up, a crimson jewel against the pallor of my skin.

I felt it immediately: the pain, the poison. It was a series of tiny sparks that ignited my nerves, the agony spreading from my finger down to my arms and onwards to the rest of my body. The poison burned, I felt it lit my veins on fire. My skin too started to shimmer, the all too familiar silvery curse spreading across my form like the first frost of winter – it was enthralling, beautiful in its own haunting way. I watched, fascinated and horrified in equal measure, as my flesh took on the hue of moonlight. The metallic sheen was blinding, and before long my vision was drenched in silver.

That was when I noticed it: the silence, the stillness. My heart had stopped its drumming, the organ withering into dead flesh.

A coldness began to seep into my bones. I felt my knees give way beneath me, the world tilting as I started to fall.

But instead of crashing onto the ground, I felt the sturdy touch of your boughs catching me. Gnarled and twisted branches cradled me in their grasp, bending and swaying to break my fall. A strange warmth enveloped me as I was slowly lowered onto the forest floor, a cocoon spun from the last threads of my consciousness. I hear your voice like rustling wind murmuring in my ears.

I surrendered to the darkness.

My last thought: you.

*

My first thought upon awakening was that this must be a dream. I blinked once, then twice and thrice, memories trickling back like raindrops from stalactites.

My limbs were heavy, exhausted from the ordeal. I took in one breath and then another. Air filled my lungs. Something felt different, a strange shift in my body and flesh. My eyes widened, realization dawning.

"My heart – " I tried to say, but then you hushed me.

I glanced at you and gasped, lips hanging agape. Tears welled in my eyes, for gone was the silver upon your bark. Your leaves were now virid and green, glossy with the morning dewdrops. Upon your branches too were tiny white flowers, blossoming like snow-pale stars. Slowly, I began to sit up, my hand reaching for my chest. My fingers traced the scar upon it, the mark of someone tearing into the space between my rib cages, plucking out the dead and withered remains of my heart.

I closed my eyes and breathed and that was when I felt it.

In the hollow of my chest, I felt *you*.

A tiny white flower where my heart once was.

Legend

Katarina Pejović

❧

My lord Ulrich is a complicated man. Complicated, and sensitive.

Even within the eye of his heart's turbulent storm, he is and remains but stone; impregnable, stalwart, impossible to sway, to compel, to make falter. His childhood tutors had informed me – with equal parts nostalgic charm and sardonic wit – that at the age of eight he could already take his precocious seat at the very table of his father's tacticians, engaging them in their intellectual jousts. At thirteen, he could best them in strategy, his mind far exceeding his still-waifish shape. By then, it had become evident that even puberty would not extend the whisper of his shoulders' expanse, nor fill the muscle of his eternally puerile gait. Now, at twenty-six, he is ruler of Iodia, commander of the known world's most disciplined and feared army, and president of the largest scientific research facility of the kingdom. Will as iron as his fist, he is our sovereign, our saviour, our beloved young king.

His sensitivity, of course, is purely physical. The heir to a long line of warrior monarchs, King Ulrich IV stands stalwart as a rapier among broadswords. Though he is powerful beyond comparison in the arts of the mind, possessing in his polymathic intellect all the world's secrets and wisdom, his frame is nothing like that of his broad-built and well muscled ancestors. Utterly incapable of exceeding his adolescent weight, my lord fares well in resembling a perpetually exhausted, bony youth – and I, having known him since he was a child, can ascertain it with confidence. Manhood simply had not treated him as generously as it did his other male relatives. With a cherubic visage sculpted with stony yet supple cheeks, thin and perpetually-scowling lips (I have always marvelled at their ability to remain unblemished by the wrinkles of his fury, or the ache of his teeth when he seizes at them in distress), a false eye, and neatly combed black hair, his likeness often comes a surprise to all those who had only heard of His Majesty, having never witnessed his likeness beyond its depictions in propaganda.

Perhaps it is because I have known him for so long that I find his form incredibly suiting. He is young, yes, young in the sense that the toils of war and constant debate have not yet folded their hours into his flesh, yet he has always struck me as shouldering the burden of a maturity which could only be made visible by the context of planets and civilizations. It is said that the very star around which our planet orbits is but a remarkably juvenile exemplar, with its cousins in distant galaxies dwarfing it in both size and tenure. In my own, as well as in the hearts of many of our people, our lord stands illuminated in much the same way, his body etched in the eclipse's shadow, but a nimble drop of ink upon the pages of history – much as our golden divinity amidst the backdrop of space – yet, in both cases, radiant and eternal in the gravity of their sustenance.

The trials and events he had endured in his short years are enough to make elders of anyone, and Ulrich IV had braced against them with elegance and sophistication. I have watched him sign treaties, forge agreements with neighbouring countries regarding resources and trade, unify an entire kingdom, and bring prosperity to both immigrants and our own poor alike. It was only natural that over time, his feats would blot out the assumed puerility of his shape, and as the people of Iodia became enchanted with the image of their gangly, stoic king, so too did his own council. Now the circle of nobles that devise new festivals and plaster the cities' streets with propaganda do not hesitate to use his native image. There is simply no need to make him look broader, more handsome, or more 'dignified' than he already is. His young face is all the dignity this kingdom could ever need.

My own place in the great puzzle that is his kingdom is a cacophony of contradictions. I know more than the closest of his advisors, yet I have no right to advise him. I am privy to his most intimate conversations, yet I am never to speak of them. I have seen him at his most capricious, his most crestfallen and distraught, yet I was never allowed to publicly comfort him. Lowly in status yet his nearest in proximity; never brushing against his official retinue, yet always marching to the pendulum swinging of his gait during his sporadic expeditions beyond the castle walls. My name, unlike that of all the other figures of his bureau, is rarely spoken; yet my physical likeness is well known by tabloid columnists and spies alike. I am his companion, his bodyguard, his only true friend.

I have long since learned that diplomacy is but a ravenous stage for a game whose stakes are far greater than my own capacity for its comprehension; the final means of its cannibalistic maw being none other than war. Every player upon the rhizomic expanse of its flesh – paid in the lives of the poor, the downtrodden, the oppressed – stands resolute, the great expanse of their visions centered upon my very lord, seeking to own him. It comes as no surprise that I find the answer to my own telos not in wielding power, but in being a power to be wielded; wielded and owned by him.

"Do you recall how we met?" I would often say, usually in the night hours when we are alone, as I change him out of his formal wear. The clothes would slip off his frail body like autumn leaves. "I know my lord was very young at the time, but I remember it fondly all the same."

"Of course," he would reply, his voice addressing me without its usual sternness. This was, itself, a game – a dialogue, a script. The words may change, but this rehearsal of our bond remained stretched taught in its web, each core memory a dull tone of gravity upon its suspension.

"It was near my seventh birthday," my lord continued. "Father had taken me to the battleground, back when we were still at war with the Harathuns. I spotted your wounded self by an oasis. You were attempting to treat yourself with the desert's water."

"I was seventeen, and an orphan. My life had no purpose back then. I felt no allegiance to the Harathun lands, and so when I saw you – the heir to the Iodian throne – I felt no anger, even though it was an Iodian who nearly killed me."

The fact that I was a Harathun by birth often brought him discomfort and guilt. It was why I always immediately followed by own exposition with: "And I am a proud Iodian now, under you, my lord."

By this time in our little game, he would be fully dressed. He would turn to me and place his hands behind his back – a signal I acknowledged well by bowing to one knee. I would close my eyes and feel his slender hand touch my forehead, heart aching with my foremost sin of pride.

"And I am proud to be your king, Wolfgang."

Wolfgang was not my birth name – no Harathun had ever been called by such obviously Iodian syllables. I had willingly shed my original moniker behind in the sand and the oasis water, completely muddied by my blood and pus.

It was, of course, my lord who had named me. Wolfgang was the name of his favourite childhood possession – a stuffed toy of a grey wolf, native to those faraway lands his family had purloined all their naming conventions from, even though its civilization had long since been relegated only to museums and history books. I adore it as I adore my new home, my clean bed, the clean water that flows through my dorm, and the exacting blades, rifles, drones, and arms I used to silence Ulrich's enemies. I have lived through nine of his assassination attempts to date. Vain as I am, I like to think that the reason they were 'attempts' were because of my presence and skill.

"Do you remember what your party had said, back then?" I'd ask, hungry to relieve the event. "What their alarmed voices had whispered to your father?"

At this point, he would press a pale thumb into his aching, stubborn lips, and mull over which impression to give.

"I recall that they glanced back at him, saying that they had found a Harathun youth – a young soldier, by the looks of it. 'Shall we dispose of him?' they asked him. It took him some time to reply."

"He turned to you," I would press on.

"Your memory serves you well, Wolf." The invocation of my nickname would always set me ablaze. "My father then turned to me, yes, and said: 'Look upon that pitiful creature. If he is allowed to live, he will certainly seek revenge. You can tell just by his musculature alone that he is a fine soldier. A swatted fly that would rise again and again.'" His voice would become even softer as he continued, "It was then that I told him to spare you. 'Father,' I said. 'Let my birthday present come early this year. I shall take him as my friend. Let me protect him and let him protect me in turn.'"

A snide smirk would climb his lips every time he retold the story.

"I was such a pampered child. He submitted to my will without question. Perhaps that is why I am so greedy now."

These private conversations we would have – murmuring our true desires, ambitions, anxieties and hopes – had become scarce, as of late. It had been so long since we even indulged ourselves in this manner, rehearsing the very moments in our friendship that administered its cooling salve upon our otherwise weary responsibilities.

Though the war with the Harathuns had long since ended, Iodia is not without political unrest. The quest for the Frost still rattles all the neighbouring countries, and Iodia's foremost competitor – the city-state of Kiro – remains vigilant in its attempts to annex its numerous land claims. It was Ulrich III who heralded this kingdom's lust for the stone, and it is his son now who bears the weight of fifty million screaming chicks – he the mother bird who must satiate their gaping mouths with promises of colossal fortune. It was in Frost that the two of us had forged our bond, for it was in its name that King Ulrich III waged war with the Harathuns. It was for Frost now that the late king's son toiled tirelessly through long nights; I accompanying him with restless eyes so accustomed to darkness.

"Our men are doing well," he says as he works. It is the first time I've heard his voice the entire day. "Port Sirene has repelled nine attacks with no casualties among them. The gods favour our royal name, it seems."

His voice – always soft, always pensive – is slightly obscured by the sound of his fingers clacking against the keyboard. I am uncertain why he still uses an older model for his network. His operating system is not even capable of linking to a thought-responsive implant – one operates it by manually dragging and pinching the holographic screen.

There is a long pause, made longer still by the twitching of his bony fingers. I observe them, flitting like pollinating bees over the letters, in watchful silence.

His nails have grown, I remark to myself. I should cut them for him soon.

Finally, he speaks.

"Kiro's army has been licking its wounds for some time now. We must take the quarry before they heal. They have done well in stalling our attempts thus far at the port."

"They may be forced to surrender if the quarry is captured," I add. "It's the largest source of Frost in the area – second only to the impact crater."

Even the way my lord nods is regal.

"We must take the quarry," he repeats. "And after that move swiftly to the crater."

At last, his frail hands eject from their study, the force swivelling his hovering chair to face me. He meets my gaze with a resolute yet cryptic gleam.

"Some sons carry on the legacies of their fathers," he hisses. "Others abandon them and carve their own paths. I acknowledge my father's ambition. His desire for the crater can be felt so strongly here, in these chambers, where he slept each night during his reign. The closer we come to our prize, the more I can smell it – in the air, in the dust, in my skin. It lingers on me like my own sweat, Wolf. Such a savage, mournful scent. It's pitiful."

I take a step forward to reach for him, but he halts my gait with a dismissive rapping of his knuckles against the fullness of his seat. I return to my perch and motion with my brows for him to continue.

"Yet father's grasp of what the Frost is truly capable of was juvenile. He died when only the most primitive technologies carved from its flesh were made. He desired the crater – the womb of the mineral, the holy wound imposed upon this Earth by the meteor which carried the substance – because he thought he could harness its power. He thought if he mined this alien crystal, with the appearance so like frozen honeycombs, eventually our scientists would develop some revolutionary technology, some new inventive scion of our kingdom's longevity."

He drew breath, one hand retreating to rub his temples, and stirred in silence. Just as I had begun to wrestle with the resurging urge to hasten to his side, my lord unfurled his spine as a serpent, arching to full height.

"Do you remember, Wolfgang, the first discoveries?" he asks me, tone lilting in the very same demeanour he would adopt whenever we rehearsed our tale.

"Of course," I say. "The excitement among your people – "

"*Our* people," he insists. "Forget the vipers. Your king elevates you."

"How right you are, lord."

My heart throbs with life. The bloodthirst of my training almost longs for a disturbance in the peace, for some assassin to burst through the window just at this moment for me to rend apart, if only to convey my utter gratitude and subservience. How ironic that the product of my vocation – the security of these very walls – renders the satiation of my calling obsolete.

"I believe I even recall the headline in our reports that day," I manage through gritted teeth, forcing my mind from the iron of blood to the alien stone of Frost. "Merely being in close contact with the mineral allows for all one's devices to be replenished to the full; as the first expedition first noticed when their own batteries swelled to power."

"It was the dawning of the revolution," my lord whispers. "There was no need to exploit our own Earth's natural resources anymore. Our ancient mother, guardian of the bones of all the ancestors of all the civilizations past, upon whose very sediment we tread and build our monuments and relics… ah, what a joy it was, we all imagined, to finally let her rest. To cease our burrowing into her flesh. To let Tiamat's body be at ease, even as Kingu's blood flows through our ingenuity. Whatever Prometheus sent this living, azure corpse to us from beyond the stars, we should surely hope he is venerated in his world, and not shackled to eternal torment against the tombstone of his rebellion."

Perhaps it is his blood to be so nostalgic. Few among us today can cite diverse mythologies like Ulrich IV, his very name an emblem of a bygone era, its numerical convention a harkening to civilizations long past. But it is my lord and none other who understands the ontology of myth; our destiny to rise to its lessons or face extinction at its judgment. It is only by his erudite instruction that I know as much as I do about the gods of old – so old now, I have often remarked, that their bones too have become one with the ancestral fossils beneath us.

"Iodia ascended with that discovery. All other countries became primitive in comparison. We were enlightened." The tremors of my lord's voice cast their shadows upon his reflections. "We were naive."

"It was when it was discovered that the Frost could be used to stir a human being's access to extrasensory perception that civilization truly changed," I continue for him. "It was then that the two great churches arose – one worshipping the substance as the lifeblood of a new god, the other saving their prayers for he who sent that sent the meteor himself, whomever that Promethean archetype, as you put it, may be."

"Aye, and we know more than ever now, in just these short two decades," he purrs. "It is why we must secure these access points. The gifts of the mind: telekinesis, telepathy, an empathy so profound one can feel a dying tree three miles away – all these must be harnessed by Iodian men and women first. If the rest of the world wishes to follow, they will have to pay us handsomely in tariffs first."

There is a soft hum as my lord dismisses the screen of his operating system, its lights winking out of existence. His voice is remarkably confident as he turns to me again and speaks.

"In the museums of today we learn about countries addicted to diamonds and gold, copper and steel, oil and coal. In the museums of tomorrow, our successors will recall a world so captivated by Frost it could hardly stagger a breath without its presence."

At last, I can no longer contain myself. I approach him, and his false eye rotates to face me, its intersecting glyphs swivelling to focus further onto my frame.

"My lord," I implore him, "you have not been sleeping well. Might I encourage you to get some rest? If you'd like, I can take your eye and clean it. You have not taken it out in some time."

My lord flares his lip defiantly at me.

"Do not concern yourself with it anymore. I doubt I'll ever retrieve it again, after the last few modifications I made. We are of one flesh now, this star-born tomb and I."

Tomb? I quell my own curiosity to investigate his choice of words further. There will always be another time, and it is best not to rile his stress further when he should truly find some solace in sleep.

The peculiar whir of his device purrs again as it focuses onto his bed. The surgery to remove his right eye to make way for a replacement of Frost was remarkably efficient and, mercifully – for my own sake, rather than for my lord's – painless. He adjusted to it in days, and the hum and clicking of his new prosthetic accompanied him ever since.

His decision to commission the sphere was not a sudden one. Ulrich IV had considered it ever since he and his closest men had reached the second level of psychic development using the mineral, under the prestigious guidance of its first scientists. The orb was a sign of trust to his people – it shielded him from any and all mental attacks, ensuring he was never manipulated through otherworldly means, and at the same time prevented him from using any of his own. It was a charming sight: the mightiest king of the mightiest kingdom, now blossoming with the development of extrasensory arts, willingly makes it so that he cannot perform any such feat himself, thereby proving to his people that he would never make them slaves of the mind. This alien stone, herald of all the mythic properties of elemental earth, was all the proof our race had needed to know that even when nature provides – sends us her angel of frozen stone to cure our ills, address our energetic dependencies, and sate our resource mismanagement – we will nevertheless reify our own inequalities, structural and economic as they may be.

Ulrich IV knew this well, determined to hasten his revolution. It would not be sudden, no, but he was convinced that it must begin with him, with his very body, to prove to our populace that it is not they who would bear the burdens of experimentation first, but he and all their elites. Before he had his prosthetic installed, my lord enacted a nation-wide ban on any manipulation of memories, along with all other deeds deemed sadistic and inhumane, and legislated the mandatory programming of all technologies utilizing the Frost to conform to these standards.

I had objected to the surgery initially. Our science had not yet discovered all the mineral's secrets, and I was deeply concerned over the possibility of side effects. It has been almost half a decade now, and my lord and all his researchers are faring just as well as they did prior to their exposure. Although it is still too early for me to be at ease, I have sworn my trepidations to silence around him.

The sound of his eye's lens focusing upon me rouses me from my wakeful dreaming.

"Wolfgang," he calls, to which I respond immediately: "My lord."

His eye rotates impatiently within its embossed socket.

"I have a request for you."

My fist finds its seat in my breast in a single, forceful salute. "Anything."

"So loyal, so kind," he laughs dryly, lip curling into a vulpine smirk. "Very well. You of all people know how greedy a king I am. I am not above making inconvenient requests."

"No request is inconvenient if it is done for you – "

"Enough, Wolf. It's far too late in the night to be so formal. We are both tired, friend, and I am about to make an unkinglike request."

I swallow my words and resume a more relaxed posture, if only for his peace of mind. My gaze follows his hand as he points towards the shelf of tomes – thin, rechargeable computers each containing thousands of manuscripts and books.

I hear the words leave his lips even before he says them.

"Read me my favourite, just like my father used to..." his voice trails as I grab the red tablet. It hums with life as I activate its screen and select the oldest fable we have recorded. As I turn to my king, who looks even more boyish and childlike in the moon's light, I instinctively imagine his six-year-old form, huddling among princely cushions with his favourite wolf toy, eagerly awaiting his father's recital of the tale of a king as godly and majestic as he.

Ulrich IV shifts over in his blankets to make room for me. I sit at the corner of the bed and load the first page.

"Sleep well, my lord," I whisper. "Sleep well and dream tonight of the city of Uruk, where the great god-king Gilgamesh lived and conquered and learned and wept and loved."

*

Iodia's rain is always torrential. Thousands of festivals and ceremonies I have overseen in my life, half of them miserable from the downpour. King Ulrich IV's funeral is no different. The gods of old, dormant amidst the shades of their ancient cultures, are crying so visibly over the loss of he who remembered them. My own tears are kept internal.

I stand beside the polished casket, my reflection stirring memories of my younger form. Fifty-three years alive have given me a mane of silver hair, countless scars, and a body of rocky muscle honed to perfection. Thirty-six years in my king's service have given me a heart, a mind, and a single, mystic eye of Frost.

He had said it was his intention to leave his eye to me in his will, even before the researchers had discovered that Frost can store a sentient being's thoughts and memories. My procedure was the first of its kind – Ulrich IV was the first person to have ever had a Frost implant, and I the first to have ever inherited another's. It is why only I know the mineral's true property. This wretched, alien crystal, so much like frozen honeycombs, can store – no, siphon, rather – a person's soul.

Of this, I am utterly convinced. Why else was it that my lord, who was of otherwise perfect health, withered away into early death? Why else was it that his eye still hummed its Faustian beat even once his heart had long ceased its own?

Why else is it that as I stand now, singing the anthem at the funeral of my beloved king, I cannot help but look upon his daughter with newfound, fatherly pride?

We share the same body now, Ulrich and I. I suspect that once the scientific community discovers the mineral's curse themselves, they will swiftly enact a nation-wide recall on its use. But politics have never been able to separate us. This sphere – as my lord had so presciently hinted to me in his chambers, whilst I was completely unawares to his greater meaning – will entomb my very soul into its prison one day, and I was determined to see to it, even if I have to send it there prematurely with my own blade; should anyone else try to prise it from my skull first.

One day, when we both feel it to be right, his daughter will know. I will not have to watch over her for him. We can and will do so together.

The adolescent Queen Frigga is every bit as regal and composed as her father. A radiant aura emanates forth from her body as she sings, equally slender hand clutching Ulrich IV's military cap over her breast. She wears an eye patch over her right eye out of respect for her father. The entire audience trembles at the sight of her ferocious yet tender performance.

She comes to me when the ceremony is at its apex.

"Wolfgang," she pronounces my name so like my lord. "Read the eulogy you showed me. It is you who should do it – no other deserves such an honour." She spies the hesitation military training cannot contain and continues, "Fear not our people's prejudices. Know that it was your lord who quelled them."

She truly is her father's daughter. She reads my invisible concerns almost as well as he.

I step up obediently to the podium and waver, veins taught against the grip of my fists. This is not how the legend unfolds, not how it inoculates its promise. It is Enkidu who dies, not Gilgamesh. Should it not be me upon the pyre, having valiantly protected him from the blight of heaven's curse upon our arrogance? Was this alien stone; this pulsating, organic mineral; this demonic evil and this divine good; the stellar virus which birthed our civilization anew – and will now surely subsume it in its endless, screeching consumption of consciousness – not fair Ishtar's Bull of Heaven?

Ulrich IV's memories cannibalize my own, the feather-light yet carnivorous touch of his thoughts arcing over the ecliptic of my mind. I had already shed my name once in the oasis, he reminds me, sloughing its weight into the sands as the serpent did in his favourite epic, becoming immortal thereby. Could I not do so again, now, spirit imprisoned in the solstice of our entwining within our eye for all eternity?

My voice is caught in my breast, refusing to emerge. There is a violent liminality thrumming in my socket, a promise of my future demise as my breath becomes archived within, layers of sediment echoing in their gravity like my king and I's little back-and-forth rehearsals of our tale.

A hand lands upon my shoulder – a hand I am aware only I can perceive, painfully in my solitude, arrogantly in my conceit. He lives in me and with me, the ephemera of his essence encoding itself in our people, in their civilization, in his descendant, in his thrumming vessel lodged in my mind; that all-familiar vortex of stone unravelling our natures and entwining us anew on Fate's loom. He is smiling proudly at his daughter. He is smiling proudly at me.

Somewhere, faintly, soft as a distant memory just forming into rebirth, I hear his voice. It calls my name and tells me to read the people their favourite legend – a tale of a great god-king who lived and conquered and learned and wept and loved.

Shadow on the Hill

Liz Williams

ଔ

I first saw the runner at dusk, on an April evening up on the Ridgeway. We'd had a cold winter that year, followed by a long period of rain, and it felt as though I had been battling against the weather for most of the year, snatching moments between chills and showers to walk the dog or attend to the garden. The cottage was chilly, damp was coming through the dining room wall, and something had chewed through a wire and plunged the ground floor into temporary darkness, resulting in an expensive and lengthy visit from the local electrician. So, when a fragile spring appeared, nervous as someone peering around a door, I thought I'd make the most of it.

It has been a bright day, with the clouds scudding across the sun, but by the end of the afternoon those clouds had disappeared, leaving a shining blue sky in their wake. I clipped on Monty's lead, put him in the car, and drove down to the car park on the edge of the Ridgeway. I could have walked the couple of miles from the village, but time was getting on, the sun was sinking, and I wanted to be back before dark. The car park was empty, so I led Monty through the new gate that the National Trust had put in and up onto the path to the hill.

The Ridgeway is a long track, sometimes said to be the oldest road in England. It follows the long line of chalk downland from Avebury to London. Its traces include Bronze Age barrows, white horses cut into the slopes, Iron Age hillforts. Prehistoric folk took the same track that I was taking today. I planned a walk of a mile or so out, then home. The Ridgeway is too long to walk in a single day.

I headed up the path, noting a little patch of creamy daffodils, incongruous on the chalky hillside. Doubtless they had escaped from someone's garden, but they cheered me, nonetheless. I left them behind and soon was high on the Ridgeway, looking down on the patchwork plain that, eventually, led to Swindon. The long slope beneath me culminated in a block of beech and oak. I contemplated it for a moment, thinking of artists like Paul Nash and Eric Ravilious, then resumed my walk, but with a slight shock I realised that I was no longer alone. Someone was running along the slope of the hill, parallel to the path. I had not spotted them before and wondered why, because they were very pale against the green grass, wearing a white garment which trailed behind them. Their head was down and their fists were clenched, but there was something odd about the head. Then I realised that the person was wearing a pointed hat. Not typical running gear, but whatever. They were certainly covering some ground. I'd never seen anyone run so fast outside the Olympics.

At this point, the dog, who had been snuffling around my feet, raised his head and took off with a sharp bark.

"Monty! Come back here!" I shouted. He had seen a pair of gulls, refugees from the coastal gales, pottering about in a field. They soared up, white against the grey sky, leaving the dog staring in bafflement. In eight years, he had never learned that birds can fly. He trotted back, shamefaced, and I looked down towards the runner, but they had gone. I could not see where they were. The hillside was empty.

Monty and I completed our walk, turning back a mile or so along the track, and returning to the car just as the sun was vanishing into the horizon's haze. But I couldn't get the runner out of my head. I think it was the pointy hat that did it. I dreamed of them that night, but it was not a significant dream, just confusion, in which sometimes I was running along the track, and sometimes they were, and sometimes we were together and the hat was not a hat at all, but a small pyramid made of chalk. This seemed ridiculous even in the dream and eventually I got up and made a cup of tea, which I took back to bed until the sun came up.

I varied the dog walks, and that morning we took one of our regular paths around the local fields. I did not forget the runner, but it was a couple of days, towards the end of the week, by the time that I returned to the Ridgeway. The weather had become milder and rather wet, so I snatched a patch of sun between showers and took the dog back along the path. I looked down the slope. The gulls were still there and had been joined by a bigger flock; they moved busily about, drumming on the ground to bring the worms up, mimicking rain.

Since it was a little earlier than our last excursion, Monty and I could walk further, and we did, heading through a patch of rainswept beech high on the ridge, then out between the sloping fields. These were dotted with hummocks, the ancient barrows of the dead who had once occupied this chalk downland and who may have been responsible for the famous white horse, some miles away at Uffington. Past Swindon, the area is known as the Vale of the White Horse, but it was much too far, and at the wrong angle, for me to see the curving form which capers across the hillside. I liked to think of it, though, as I walked past the peaceful barrows. There were no sheep so I let Monty off the lead and he did his own thing, snuffling along the base of the old hedgerows. By now, my hiking boots were smudged with wet chalk dust, but the air felt fresh and clear. I paused, took a deep lungful of it, swung my arms to loosen my shoulders, turned and saw the runner. Before I could stop him, Monty shot across the field to the runner's feet.

They were not running this time. They stood alongside one of the barrows, staring at me. I say 'they,' because the runner was rangy and tall, but I was not entirely sure that they were male. They wore a long garment of unbleached linen, rough in texture and colour, wrapped around them like grave goods (this thought made me take a step back). And the hat – it was not a hat at all, but the high, pointed shape of a bald skull.

"Where have you come from?" the runner asked. An old, rough voice; impossible still to tell the gender.

"Avebury." The conversation felt dreamlike. Somewhere, I was aware of a spark of fear, but the whole thing felt too strange for me to be truly afraid. If the person had been a man, in contemporary clothes, then perhaps I would have been. I added, "the stones."

"Ah, yes. I know the folk of the stones."

"And you?"

"From the country of the white horse. But before that, from the great river."

The skull had to be some kind of deformity, or was this person even human? As they bent to touch the little dog's head, I saw that the hairless skull had been smeared with chalk. They picked up Monty and carried him over the field. I saw watery, rheumy eyes, faded blue and red rimmed, and the sharp hollow of the cheek, a sign of missing teeth.

"There," the runner said, and set Monty down at my feet. The dog did not seem remotely perturbed.

"Your head," I said. "I do not mean to be rude. I'm curious."

The runner gave me a cautious look. "You've not seen this before?"

"No, never."

"The river tribes bind the heads of certain children, if they have been god-touched."

"Oh, I see. How do people know that a child is god-touched?"

"There will have been a sign. At my birth, the sun was eaten for part of a day."

The conversation was becoming increasingly surreal: we could not be speaking English, surely. Was the runner a ghost? I still could not determine their gender. But I could smell them: earth, sweat, a bitter herbal pungency.

"Why were you running?" I asked.

"I don't know." They looked puzzled, hurt, like a child. A cloud crossed the sun, the Ridgeway grew shadow dark. The runner said, "I have to go."

"Oh," I said, because although I was afraid, I wanted to go on talking. "Must you?"

But there was no-one there. I searched around the barrow but the field was quiet and still. The flock of gulls rose up, whirling into the wind, and flew due east. I watched them go, wondering. But there seemed nothing to link the runner and the gulls and presently I turned away, called the dog, and walked back to the car.

I spent the evening looking up the Ridgeway on the internet. There was a lot of information, but I didn't think all of it was reliable. The tribes of those days didn't write anything down, so all we really know of them came from the Romans, who were much later, and biased. There was a curious article about a Greek merchant who claimed to have sailed around the island of Britain and who was told of a great city, in the middle of Salisbury plain, devoted to Apollo, the god of the sun. I liked the thought of this – it conjured, in my mind's eye, the image of a ziggurat, the sun rising behind, its rays conquering heaven with their golden glow.

I thought this might have stemmed from some Medieval image I had once seen, but I was not sure. It was very compelling, but almost certainly wrong: there were no traces of such a temple, only the henge itself and the barrows which surrounded it. Stonehenge had not given up all of its secrets, it was true, but I did not think a 'great city' was among them.

Of head binding, there was nothing that related to this period of time. I found many accounts of the practice among the South American tribes, and some references to the Germanic: that was a little closer to home. There did not seem to have been many skulls found which had this manufactured deformity, but from what my new friend had said, the practice was not commonplace, and perhaps it was just too long ago.

I went back, of course. The very next day, but there was no sign of the runner, only the gulls wheeling and screaming above the dark ploughed earth. Monty and I walked a long way along the Ridgeway, encountering nothing stranger than a woman in a Barbour jacket with a brace of spaniels. We exchanged polite greetings; there was nothing in her face, no trace of old alarm, to show that the day had been anything but a normal one for her.

Then it rained. We all exchanged commiserations in the Post Office and the village shop. Equinoctial gales, we told each other sagely, and to be expected at this time of year. I did not mind lying in my warm bed, listening to the wind roaring about the chimneys, but I did mind the hiatus in gardening. And as I lay in bed, the house warmed by the wood burning stove, I wondered about the runner and their people. How hard had it been, in those days, to keep warm and dry? Not very easy, I should have thought, and I looked back upon them, my possible ancestors, with respect. I had visited Stonehenge several times, had seen the antler picks with which the tribes dug the holes for the great posts, and I lived close to Silbury Hill and Avebury, also man made. So much effort, so much hard labour, not for survival but to erect these enigmatic monuments. As I sank into a half sleep, I watched them, like the folk in Medieval hours speeded up, in storm and snow and sleet, in rain and fleeting summer sun, until sleep itself claimed me.

I woke to sunlight, still haunted by that ancient effort. Making a cup of tea, I let the dog out and walked around the dripping garden, the yellow heads of the daffodils bowed and bobbing in the wind. Up on the hills, cloud shadows chased and I felt a great need to get out, into the upper air. Today, we would go again to the Ridgeway.

As I turned the engine off into the sudden silence of the car park, I was conscious of a tingling sense of anticipation. There was no-one else there, and once we were up on the track and the car had fallen out of sight, the Ridgeway felt timeless. Villages and distant Swindon were lost in a haze, which I found hard to understand because the day was so clear, the stands of beeches sharp against the sky. It was with a sense of inevitability that I saw the runner.

They ran like a deer, swifter and more easily than a person should be able to run, particularly with the long garment bound up around them. I watched them weave and dip between the barrows and then suddenly out of sight. I shaded my eyes, the sun passed behind a cloud, I turned and the runner was there behind me.

"Hello," I said, though my heart was pounding. The dog was quiet, huddling against my legs.

"It is a long time since I have seen you," the runner said.

'A week, perhaps. The weather's been foul.' As though we were chatting inside the village post office.

"No," they said. "It has been years. Before the people came

down from the north." They spoke a word before 'people' but I did not catch it.

"Has there been trouble?"

"At first. At first there was war." They held up their hand, marked with red ochre and chalk, and I saw that two fingers were missing. "They brought new weapons with them. Now there is a truce. And you?"

"I'm well. Thank you." Then I said, "Can I ask – how old are you?" As soon as the words were out of my mouth, I thought, *what a stupid question.*

The runner did not appear to find it so, however, but considered it. They said,

"I came from the great river lands when I was young, when things seemed limitless to me and I thought I would never die. Then I began to feel that time was running from me, that I could glimpse my end ahead, and I needed to do more before that happened. So perhaps I am old. I am older than most of the – " and there was a name again, a name I could not hear.

"I feel the same –" I started to say, but the runner was no longer there.

After this, I decided that I would come to the Ridgeway on the following day, too. Perhaps earlier, perhaps at dawn. Each time I had seen the runner, it had been close to twilight and I wondered if it might only be the liminal times in which they appeared. I would try dawn, then return at the end of the day if I did not see the runner.

So next morning I rose early, gave Monty a quick walk around the garden while it was still dark, then sent him gratefully enough to his basket and drove to the Ridgeway. As I pulled into the car park, the sky was lightening and once I was up on the track, with the last stars fading, it was clear that it was going to be a fine day. Venus gleamed but was quickly gone, banished by the sun as it came up in gold over the horizon. I walked slowly down the track, enjoying the silence, but it was soon broken.

I heard shouts, up ahead. The noise stopped me in my tracks, I could see someone running down the crest of the Ridgeway, not the person I knew. He wore a brown cloak, a stocky man with a thick beard. His mouth was open and he stumbled, then he went down. I could see him trying to struggle to his feet. Other men ran from within the grove of beeches: they wore grey, they were all grey, faces and hair, except for their panda eyes. A second later I realised that they were covered in chalk, their eyes circled with rings of charcoal. Ignoring me, they ran to the man and one of them thrust a bronze spear like a great leaf into his throat. He kicked once and lay still.

I felt my head thud and pound. I had seen violence before – but a couple of fights in street or pub, never a killing. I think I made a sound. One of the killers looked up, sharply, and saw me. He gave a shout, pointed down the track. And then he was running, not like the deer-stride of my friend, but as fast as a fit man could run and the spear flashed bright in the sun as he threw it and I could not move, I had no time.

Someone was between me and the spear bearer. I heard the spear strike, a whistle, cut abruptly off. The runner was there, sinking to their knees. Their white coned head was bowed over the shaft. I heard myself shouting, *no, no, no.* Then the spear bearers, the dead man, the spear itself were gone and only I and the runner remained on the Ridgeway. Blood was coming from the runner's mouth as they crumpled.

I dropped down beside them. The blood was only a trickle and then it powdered into dust, into chalk. The runner was young again, a sharp planed face, a hawk's face, brown beneath the chalk and the red-rimmed eyes were as blue as the sky. The oddly shaped skull was shaved.

"Don't worry," the runner said, rasping. "This happened long before you walked this way. It will happen again. The world turns, that's all."

"Will I see you again?" I said.

"I'm always here." And then the runner was gone, blinked out of sight as the sunlight powered through the beeches and lit the track.

*

I went back to the Ridgeway on the following day. I left Monty behind and my hands were shaking on the wheel as I parked the car. I had not slept well the previous night, but it was a beautiful afternoon, the spring sky pale and clear, cloudless as the sun sank over Bristol and the Severn far away. I waited for a long time up on the track, avoiding the beeches, watching the barrows, but the runner was not there. Then, as the sun blazed down, I saw a faint figure gleam beneath the turf: the shadow of a ghost of a chalk figure, outlined in white. Once, perhaps, it would have gleamed from the hillside, but it had become overgrown and faded: a human figure, with a long staff, like the Man of Wilmington far to the east. Its narrow head was pointed.

Had my runner ever been human, I wondered, or some spirit, conjured out of the land? Some spirit brought from the east after the Ice Age, when Britain was still joined to the Continent, before a great river was swallowed by the sea and became the smaller Thames? It was too long ago and I would never know. But I knew that I would come to the Ridgeway again, at sunset and sunrise, to see if there might be a person, ancient of days, running endlessly over the land, a shadow on the hill.

About the Authors

☙

Maria Hummer is a British-American writer of fiction and screenplays. Her stories have appeared in *The White Review*, *Wasafiri*, *Devil's Lake*, and more. She is the screenwriter behind prize-winning short film 'He Took His Skin Off For Me' (which has altogether over 10 million views online) and many others. When she is not writing, Maria can be found working as a social media guru for The College of Psychic Studies in London.

'The Watchers' was inspired by a real stone circle in England and the legend attached to it about how the stones had once been men.

Sasha Ravitch spends her days as a consultant-practitioner and professional writer who loves few things more than a good monster and a bad human. She regularly appears on podcasts and at conferences, and has a modest handful of publications both showcasing non-fiction and fiction-work. Ravitch spends her free time spinning starlight and constellating stories from the floor of the ocean or a sunny rock in the river, and reading and writing weird worlds and even stranger spirits into existence.

Wendy Ashley lives in Somerset, works in a library, and writes contemporary fantasy. She has a love for the countryside and a long-held interest in folktales and mythology which feeds into her writing. She has an MA in Creative Writing from Bath Spa University and is working on a novel set in the landscape of the West of England. 'A Fox's Heart' is her first published story.

'A Fox's Heart' was inspired by the folktale trope of the external soul, where a character removes their heart and hides it in order to be invulnerable to harm.

DEMIAN LAMONT is a writer from Mexico City.

TRISH MARRIOT was born. That definitely happened. And, by the power of Sekhmet, is still here now. Everything in between is a bit of a blur, memories triggered by photographs, music, books, films and places. In winter she can be found behind the bar at a local music venue. In the summer she goes camping in her hand-painted 3m bell tent and crochets quietly in a corner till its time to dance. The stories form in her head without cease, living, breathing, constantly evolving, but this is the first time one has escaped in any kind of coherent form and allowed her to nail it down. It Would.Not.Shut.Up till she did. The next one got out already so the die is cast. #tellthestory

IVY SENNA, born and raised in Thailand, is an occultist, astrolater, and witch. From the dirt of the earth to the deep sea and deep space, she is a lover of all things eldritch and monstrous.

Her piece, 'Tiny White Flowers', is inspired by her love for the prunus spinosa— the blackthorn trees which adorn the rolling hills of Somerset, a place she calls home, for the time being. Ivy can be found online @ivy.crowned on Instagram and via her blog at uponthealtar.com

Katarina Pejović is a religious studies scholar investigating the connections between oral folklore, saint veneration, and traditions of magic and witchcraft across diverse cultural contexts. Her short stories draw on her lifelong passion for the folk traditions of the Balkan peninsula, as well as her ongoing studies in cross-cultural examples of ancestral veneration and sorcerous engagement. Both her academic and creative works seek to explore the complicated relationships between the petitions, prayers, and conjurations of living devotees and the ephemeral, echoing responses of liminal Others.

Her contribution, 'Legend', is a sci-fi exploration of the core themes of the Epic of Gilgamesh, illustrating the necromancy of our cultural god-kings of myth—and how their very humanity forms the basis of their enduring relevance in stone.

Liz Williams is a science fiction and fantasy writer living in Glastonbury, England, where she is co-director of a witchcraft supply business. She has been published by Bantam Spectra (US) and Tor Macmillan (UK), also Night Shade Press and appears regularly in *Asimov's* and other magazines. She has been involved with the Milford SF Writers' Workshop for over 25 years, and also teaches creative writing at a local college for Further Education.

Milton Keynes UK
Ingram Content Group UK Ltd.
UKHW010824110724
445228UK00001B/2